Consuming the Muse

- erotic tales -

by

AstridL

First published in Australia
by
RAGING AARDVARK PUBLISHING
http://ragingaardvark.com

Copyright © 2013 AstridL
All rights reserved.

ISBN: 0-9871383-5-9
ISBN-13: 978-0-9871383-5-4

Cover Image and Artwork: © 2013 Sharon Ratheiser
Cover Design by Sessha Batto

Raging Aardvark Publishing.
Brisbane, Australia
Established 2012

Consuming the Muse is a collection of erotic tales flirting with time, space and the senses, on a woman's journey through Eros. Some of these stories may titillate, some may make you think.

Sensual: of the senses or the indulgence of appetite: fleshy, sensory; devoted to, or preoccupied with, the senses or appetites; voluptuous...

Food, drink, Dionysian indulgences, passion, obsession dominate AstridL's collection of erotic stories. Some are *amuse-bouches*, 'By the Skin of the Nose,' and others a groaning-board of orgiastic excess. I loved 'Dancing with Chopsticks' and chuckled through, 'It's All in the Nose.' Appetites of all sorts are bound together as the most essential of human need, and it's done with intelligence and wit, with twists that lend piquancy in unexpected places and ways. Interspersing these are the palate cleansing, 'Soul Kill' and, notably, the gentle, sad, 'Just Lunch.' What struck me as I read through the book was the growing maturity of voice in the stories, playful, naughty, stunning, turning thoughtful, detailed, beautifully crafted. It's an interesting read, complex and varied. I hope you enjoy it. ~ *Helena Settimana.*

AstridL has a wonderful way of combining the art of arousal with the art of cooking. Her writing mixes both subjects in such a beautiful way as to arouse all of one's senses at once. What an incredible feat and such a luscious treat for her readers. ~ *Jamie Joy Gatto* (Editor-in-Chief of *Mind Caviar*)

ACKNOWLEDGEMENTS

Several stories have appeared, some slightly differently, online and in print in *Mind Caviar*, *Ophelia's Muse*, *Scarlet Letters*, *The Erotic Woman*, *Travelrotica for Lesbians #2* (Alyson Books, US), *Five Minute Fantasies - Seriously Sexy 1 - Ultimate Sins* (Xcite Books, UK), *In My Bed Magazine* (Canada), *The New Black Lace Book of Women's Sexual Fantasies* (edited by Mitzi Szereto for Virgin Books, UK), *The Summer of '76* (Stringybark Books, Australia), *Back Burning* (IP, Australia), and as mobile downloads at Ether Books.

'Matilda's Waltz' was inspired by 'Waltzing Matilda' by Banjo Paterson (1864-1941).

'Butter Cup' was inspired by Austrian, Elfriede Vavrik, who at 79 published her autobiography, *Nacktbadestrand* (Ullstein, 2010), to critical acclaim.

I am grateful to Jamie-Joy Gatto, Editor-in-Chief of *Mind Caviar*, and Helena Settimana for their support.

My thanks to Sharon Ratheiser, for allowing me to use her artwork in this collection. It also appears on the cover. I also thank Jake Moss for his editorial eye.

My thanks to my husband and to my Swedish brother, for believing in me and my stories and giving me the space in which to write them.

AstridL, Vienna, May 2013
http://www.astridl.blogspot.com

To the Muse

CONTENTS

Coming for the Muse

The only other time my mother spoke to me about sex was when I was fifteen. It was an effort to demystify the contents of my womb with the help of illustrations in my zoology book. I don't have memories of ever having been told to keep my fingers out of *there*, although I do recall how I told my two-year old daughter that one did not do *that* with people around. And although I cottoned on later to what he was getting at, I'm sure that my mother, one of those women who eventually gets everything right, never wanted to go into the reasons for Mick Jagger singing, 'I can't get no …'. Or maybe she knew that in the end it was not satisfaction that was the name of the game.

All these jumbled thoughts played with my mind as I waited for 'men pause' to strike. My ovaries were having what I thought was their final fling, yet I still wondered why I was suddenly in such a state of enduring arousal.

I told my muse, but his reaction did not solve the problem, if problem there were.

'Are you still horny?' he asked me before I left.

'I think I'll be horny forever.'

'Music,' he said.

My muse is a man. Who else could coax the unspeakable from within my core to my breast and down the length of my arm, to my right hand, through my fingers, the pen, the keys, to the page? Music. Yes. But he wasn't around and it wasn't really about him. It was about me.

More and more, I wanted to explore. I would have dreams of dancing naked in a roomful of dildos. There were black ones and red ones, purple, yellow; there were big ones and curved ones, ones with glitter and with little appendices: what they all had was smiles on their dickheads. I wanted books on my shelves about cock, clit and cunt, but I wanted nice covers.

Just like Peter Pan in the film, *Hook,* when he'd become too old to fly, I'd missed the sixties. But it wasn't too late to play with the forbidden. Four-letter words: Fuck was one I had started to say aloud, but only when swearing; then there was cock as in peak, cunt as in hunt, clit as in split. And oh, so much more in the name of love. I wanted to play with anal and bang, blow, buns and bush, butt, come and slit. I wanted oils and creams, candles and lubes. I wanted to drown in an orgy of the senses. I wanted to learn how to masturbate. Do a course, start from scratch. I didn't want mail order. I wanted someone to take me in hand. A shop. Friendly staff. I had questions to ask.

I'd sent an email from the town of Calvin in Switzerland where I lived. No sex shops in the city? One. Two. Maybe more tucked away in the red-light area behind the station. I scuttled in once for a look and scuttled out again with my clandestine purchase of pink pleasure balls. A present from me to me on my 52nd birthday. My mother's day gift was the trip to New York and a tube to the Lower East side. *Babes in Toyland.* The musical? No way.

My heart was beating as I pushed open the door. Over 18. You betcha. So why did I feel nervous? Wow! It was gorgeous. So was she. Like the girl next door. I've always had a soft spot for tomboyish redheads. From my Pippi Longstocking days, I guess. At the threshold, I let slip the coat of being a wife, a mother from my shoulders. I only had that afternoon in the store. It was now or never. I had to do the necessary research. I was a writer, a lover, and I was going to learn how to write erotica. My head spun. It was gorgeous, I felt dizzily free.

'So you made it?' she said. 'Come. Put your bag down and I'll show you around.'

'Do you have the same size, but without the vanilla taste?' The words floated across from a table of dildos. A voluptuous black woman wistfully stroked a large curved purple number and I couldn't help staring.

'Do you want to start with the dildos?' the redhead said.

I put my bag down and shook my head. It was spinning. Then I blurted: 'I don't know what I want. This is my first time. Can you show me...the Hitachi wand?'

The redhead raised one eyebrow and smiled. She was gentle and pretty. Freckles sprinkled her nose. She picked up the biggest vibrator I had ever seen. Now this wasn't difficult since I had only seen the mail order ones intended for easing pain in the neck region. I could never get that 'wand' inside me. Then I realised that perhaps that was not the main intention. The redhead turned it on.

'Do you have something a little more...discreet? In size and in sound?'

She showed me a tiny finger cap. 'It comes with its own little purse to slip on a belt.'

I could just see myself travelling with my bum bag and the mini vibe purse. 'Is it any good?'

She turned it on. It gave a low buzz. 'I need something a little more powerful myself,' she confided.

'Looks fine to me,' I said. 'I'm just a beginner. I'll take the purple one.' Purple seemed to fit my mood perfectly.

'There are books there. A wonderful one called *Simply Clit.*'

'I was looking for *The Best of,*' I said. 'I can't get those in Geneva.'

'There are no sex shops?'

'Not like this. I bought some pink balls though. They were the only things discreet enough. It was a shop in the middle of town,' I added hastily.

'And how are they?'

'The balls?'

The redhead nodded.

'I tried them once. I didn't dare bring them.'

'X-rays at the airport,' she said and shook her head.

'Oh my God. Wearing the balls and then having them ding as you go through the controls.' I started to giggle.

The redhead giggled with me. 'There's worse,' she said. 'Wear a harness to JFK and see where that gets you.'

'I'm not that far yet.'

She smiled and gave me a postcard. 'There's a masturbation marathon this Sunday. You're welcome to come.'

I took the card. A forties-type playmate, who reminded me of my mother, sat atop a Hitachi wand, stroking her cheek with a daisy. *Masturbate-A-Thon.* 'I'd love to,' I said. 'But I fly out that night. I'm here for a meeting. Work.'

The redhead nodded. 'Another time then.'

'I'll just have a look at the books before I go.' I didn't want to leave, but I had to. There was no pocket of time for me to return I bought three anthologies and the purple finger fiddler. It was a start. When the mind loosens, the vagina luxuriates.

Back in Geneva, the Earth Mother was calling. I had to nurture, care for and hold those I love. But I would fantasize, and my cunt would drip with Tahitian pearls as my muse fondled my puckering butthole with creamy fresh butter, his fingers slipping so gently, easing, stroking and poking, making way for his cock so eager to sink home, and thrusting me beyond space and time.

Then came the eleventh day of September. I emailed the redhead. She said she was safe.

I sleep in chunks now of three or four hours. I do not have headaches, but the Earth Mother in me has to learn once again as I try to pretend I'm still this side of bruised. And so I curl up like the child I once was, hiding my hands between my thighs, seeking safety and comfort in this foetal position. It is then that my fingers begin their own life and trace gently to dip into my moist inner reaches, and I rub and I rub until I find sleep.

It's All in the Nose

Dr Stanley Higginbothom, GP, needed a break. Not only was it time for his well-earned holiday away from the sniffles and sneezes of summer colds that persisted on from the last winter and even ones before, he also wanted time away from Northern England to devote to his— olfactory research. Dr Stanley Higginbothom had a big nose. This appendage put him in good stead to be able to smell a rat, or even the roses, and the latter was what he now needed. He wanted to go somewhere nobody knew him, where he could be himself and reflect on his future. He had just turned forty. He would fly to Salzburg and take a local bus to the tiniest of towns where he had a fortnight's booking.

Gerlinda Schrittesser straightened the sheets in the double-bed room on the second floor of Hotel Seeblick. She was happy to have found a job she had been able to hold down for over a month. Chamber maid. She could take her time, even day dream a little, and the curious ailment that afflicted her from time to time now could bother no one at all. It had bothered so many in the past and, although a source of great pleasure had, in a sense, confined her to a life alone.

Hotel Seeblick was preparing to host a wedding, and apart from the room booked by Dr Higginbothom, all the others were booked for the wedding guests. There would be music and dancing and balloons. Gerlinda smiled at the thought of the balloons; dozens of white ones floating up to the sky, little strings hanging down – she giggled. It reminded her of an old film where Woody Allen stood poised in a white head-to-toe jumpsuit, a sperm not anxious to take the plunge as a young man moved closer to a young woman in *Every Thing You always Wanted to Know About Sex But Were Afraid to Ask*. Gerlinda started laughing out loud, then began trembling and gripped the bed head with one hand. Suffused by the delicious quivering that always came, and then released her in a final *ahhh* following the buildup of her laughter, she dropped to the bed. She rocked a little, then went to the bathroom and wiped herself gently between the legs. It would not do to leave a trace in the room of a guest, a doctor; even if he was English. She giggled again. Stop now, she said to herself. Control yourself.

Control was something Dr Higginbothom knew all about. He was forever trying to control the slight flaring of his nostrils whenever a delicate smell wafted his way. He was pleased with his booking in Hotel Seeblick, although there wasn't a lake in Fucking. Odd name for a village, he thought as he checked in to the hotel. He'd heard that the town was beloved amongst British tourists; it's only claim to fame being its name, which in German rhymed with 'booking', or 'looking'. But he had managed to secure the last room. There was a wedding, they'd said. A wedding, he sighed. That would be something he would never see, as a groom at least. His large nose always seemed to get in the way of any *rapprochement*.

Dr Higginbothom pushed open the door to his room. It was quite spacious for such a small hotel. He touched the bed to feel – a waterbed. He put down his suitcase and lay on the bed, moving his body, feeling a give as he rolled from one side to the next. His left nostril flared, then his right. Delight! What a delicate scent. He sat up slowly and looked around. No one. But this wasn't some spray to perfume the room. This was what he had always dreamed of. *Sensa di donna*! His nostrils flared, almost like wings. I must find her.

The knock at the door made him stand up.. He ran two fingers down his nose to redress his nostrils, and opened the door.

'Excuse me,' Gerlinda said, 'the towels.' She went to the bathroom.

Stanley followed her, his nostrils now living a life of their own. In such proximity to the exciting scent, they were going wild. Gerlinda turned and looked at Stanley's nose and the two little wings either side. 'Oh dear,' she said and started giggling.

'Yes, I know,' Stanley said sadly. 'They always do that,' meaning both his nostrils and the reaction of young women when they saw them in action.

'You are a doctor?' she said through her giggles.

'Yes,' said Stanley, his hand over his nose. How can I feel so sad and still think I'm in heaven, he thought.

Gerlinda started shaking, almost convulsing. 'Can...you...help...me?' she stuttered as she pushed past him and flopped onto the bed. Stanley followed, led by his nostrils.

'Wait!' she *ahhed*. 'Wait, wait, wait, wait! Oh yes!'

Stanley stood by the bed and took her pulse. It was racing. That was not unusual. But this young woman seemed to have a problem of a more unconscious nature. 'Does this happen often? he asked in his best doctoral tone.

Gerlinda nodded.

Stanley reflected. He had heard of orgasm leading to laughter, but this seemed to be the other way round. 'Do you not think something is missing? ''I do miss a cuddle, if you must know. Someone's hands touching me. Someone's lips.'

Stanley breathed in deeply. He was a GP, a professional, but he was on holidays. And after all, this was Fucking, at least by name. And maybe he could help this sweet young thing.

'I think I'm coming again,' Gerlinda whispered haltingly, 'I can't help it.'

'It's my nostrils,' Stanley said.

'Don't be sad,' Gerlinda said, her giggles colliding. 'What a wonderful gift. How often can I go on like this?' She started shaking again. 'It's wearing me out.'

Dr Stanley Higginbothom took off his tie and threw it across the room. He then laid himself down on the waterbed, his weight tipping him closer to Gerlinda. He nestled his shoulder against her head and stroked her hand. Her trembling stopped. 'Just stay there,' he said, breathing in deeply and safe from her sight, 'If I might try an experiment?'. Gerlinda nodded. 'Just some touching, gently, so you don't see me, so you don't laugh.' She turned her back to him and he gently peeled her straps from her shoulders. His hand ventured around her to cup her left breast. He could feel her heart pounding. Gently does it, he thought, and lowered his face, letting his nose caress the back of her neck. Gerlinda stirred and pulled his hand past her bunched up skirt through the top of her panties into a moist jungle of wetness.

Stanley sighed. Heaven in Fucking or fucking in heaven. If that only could be next, he thought as a second appendage began to swell almost to the degree of his excited nostrils. 'Have you lived here long?' he whispered.

'In Fooking?'

'We say, *fucking* in English'.

'I know,' Gerlinda said and started to giggle.

'Not yet,' said Stanley, smoothing her skirt down below her legs, his nose following, sniffing, almost drinking in her essence.

'I want to see you,' Gerlinda said.

'That will spoil the experiment,' Stanley whispered.

'Not your nose,' she said, 'down there.' She turned and pulled at the zip of his trousers, and stared at the bulge. 'Ohh,' she said. 'It's true.'

'What's true?'

'What they say about noses and cocks.'

Stanley pursed his lips.

'I wasn't just laughing at your nose. I was excited to see such a big one,' she said.

And before he could reply, Gerlinda pulled down his briefs and ran her nose over his now swollen cock.

Stanley was taken by surprise. 'Have you..?'

'I've never smelt one before,' Gerlinda said. 'Can I taste?'

'Stanley cleared his throat. 'Taste is 85% smell,' he said in a reasoned voice, but it was too late. Gerlinda's tongue slithered from his balls and flicked over a tiny white drop on the tip of his penis.

'Sperm,' Gerlinda moaned. 'Woody Allen.'

'I beg your pardon,' Stanley moaned.

'It's a joke,' Gerlinda said in a muffled voice. Then she took him deep into her mouth and sucked, sucked.

'Please stop. I like it so.' Stanley said, his fingers tangled in her hair. 'This isn't fair.'

Gerlinda sat up and with her eyes closed took his head in her hands and rolled onto her back. 'Don't you want to see if it's true?' she said. 'The 85%?'

Stanley smiled weakly. Never had he had such a direct invitation. He burrowed his head between her legs, his nostrils lapping, then his tongue. Then he sucked, slurped through an orgy of her juices until he felt her convulsing, coming, exploding in his mouth.

'Yes!' she cried. 'Yes, yes, yes, yes!'

'And now for some real fucking,' Stanley heard himself say and straddled Gerlinda, who lay all the while with her eyes closed and a look of pure pleasure on her face. It was true, she thought. The nose has it.

Stanley pumped and thrust and fondled her breasts, hovered and sniffed her chest and her shoulders. Gerlinda felt herself coming again.

'Doctor,' she moaned. She opened her eyes. She did not laugh. Stanley stroked her cheek with one hand.

Spent, he rolled over by her side and held her in his arms. Gerlinda sighed. 'I'll be fired again,' she said.

The music outside was getting louder and words became clearer as Bruno Mars sang from a distant stereo: 'I think I want to marry you.'

'Do you,' Gerlinda said.

'I do,' said Stanley.

The next Saturday, Dr Stanley Higginbothom and Gerlinda Schrittesser were married in the Austrian village of Fucking. Hotel Seeblick did not fire Gerlinda, but the staff were relieved that she would be taking up new duties somewhere in the north of England as a doctor's wife.

They presented her with flowers, cream roses, and they gave Stanley a metal sign bearing the name of the village where it had all begun. In the duty-free shop at Salzburg airport, Dr and Mrs Stanley Higginbothom were elated to find a DVD of an old Woody Allen film.

.

Cherry Strudel

Lucia loved food. She loved the look, the taste, the feel, the smell, even the sound of it as she kept it that second longer in her mouth before she let it slip away. Maybe the reason she loved sex was because the first time she was seduced, her hands were deep in some pearly dough.

Lucia worked in a restaurant kitchen, learning, among other things, to knead the dough for strudel. Bruno, the Austrian cook, had convinced the restaurant owner that strudel—not just apple strudel, but cherry strudel, plum strudel and even rhubarb strudel—would be novel additions to the dessert menu of *The Hungry Taste Bud*.

Bruno was an artist and like most artists preferred to get on with the creative part, leaving the routine of preparing the strudel dough to the kitchen help. Yet he always kept an eye the preparation of the dough.

'250 gm of flour, Lucia. Mix it with one eighth of a litre of water.' Bruno paused in his instruction as the girl in her white wrap-around apron gingerly measured the flour, tipped it into a bowl and added the liquid.

Lucia glanced up at the man. She needed him to give her time, time to see that it didn't matter if some of the flour powdered onto the marble top counter.

'Add two tablespoons of oil...that's it...just pour it on...one whole egg, now...careful with the shell. Take the wooden spoon...stir it all about at first.'

His voice rolled low as Lucia stirred the dough, her silky black chin-length hair swaying to the motion of her arm; her eyes fixed on the changing matter in the bowl.

'And now, Lucia, just a coffee spoon of vinegar and a pinch of salt.'

She added the last with a flourish and a satisfied smile.

'Take the spoon out now—this is where you need to use your hands—if you want to make a really good strudel dough.'

Lucia scraped off the wooden spoon and watched as Bruno sprinkled more flour on the counter.

'So it won't slip,' he said.

She pushed a strand of hair from her forehead with the back of her hand causing tiny speckles of flour to fall and trace her jawbone. As he lifted the mass of dough from the bowl and began kneading, a faintly sour scent rose to her nostrils. She gazed at the long, strong and even movements of his hands as he kneaded the dough until it had a pearly sheen.

'It has to look and feel like silk,' he said. 'Why don't you go on for a while…just to get the feel of it.'

Lucia nodded, wiped her hands on her apron and plunged both hands into the dough.

'Push down, Lucia. Push with both heels of your hands. Draw the dough back with your fingers. Keep the rhythm.'

Lucia pulled and pushed and pulled and pushed. It felt as though her whole body was moving in harmony. As she leant forward to push with the heels of her hands across the counter, her knees bent so slightly in a rolling motion, causing the hem on the back of her dress to rise with the swell of her shoulders bearing down on the dough.

Bruno took a step back to gaze at the hypnotic movement. The only sound that could be heard was the cool flap-flap against the marble and the sound of rhythmic breathing.

Lucia kept on kneading, eyes half-closed. She felt a hand brush a trace of flour from her cheek as another glided from her shoulder to rest on her hips. Lucia kept on kneading. She sensed the knot at the back of her dress surrender as the hands crept beneath the loosened cloth.

'Hush,' Bruno whispered in her ear. 'Keep the same pace. It's good for the dough.'

Tiny shivers rippled up from somewhere deep inside her as the hands cupped her breasts and a finger and thumb gently tugged at her nipples to the rhythm of her kneading.

'This will be a wonderful strudel dough, Lucia.' Bruno's voice was softly hoarse. 'But we must put it aside and cover it ... then let it rest for half an hour.'

Lucia turned, her hands behind her back tightening the knot and drawing the white cotton of her dress tautly across her breasts.

'And what shall we do in that half hour?' she asked.

Bruno stroked a finger down her cheek and brushed her lips with his. 'The strudel, Lucia. We have to finish it.'

Her palms warm and her breasts flushed, Lucia's brown eyes searched Bruno's.

'We'll need half a kilo of those dark red cherries, 60 gm of butter, 120 gm of bread crumbs and about 250 gm of sugar,' he said.

Lucia stroked a hand over her hip and turned towards the cooler chamber where the fruits and vegetables were stored.

'Half a kilo of cherries,' she whispered.

The cherries lay in a basket, plump and red, a red so deep it was almost black. She took a pair and slipped it over her left ear. She took a single cherry, placed her lips against it to feel its shine, then sank her teeth slowly into the flesh. Juice trickled down her lower lip as she smelled the rich full scent. She held the stone in her mouth to suck the last of its pulp and, puckering her lips, spat the stone into the bin.

'Lucia,' Bruno called. 'I'll show you how to pip the cherries.'

She came towards him, the basket propped on her left hip, the cherry earring laughing at him like her dark brown eyes.

'I shall wash them first,' Lucia said and emptied the basket into the enamel sink filled with cold water. She felt Bruno's eyes upon her as she swished the bobbing cherries about in the water. She tried to ignore him but inside she was throbbing with a strange excitement. When she had strained the cherries, she turned to Bruno and looked him straight in the eye. 'What now?'

'Ah, Lucia. We must remove all the stones.' With a small kitchen knife he made a cut down the cherry. 'Now take it and open gently, so as to keep it whole. Then pluck the stone.'

A flush rose from her neck to her cheeks as Bruno gently opened the fruit. They stood side by side; the tall blond man and the slim dark-haired girl; they worked the cherries until the fruit was ready. The fresh smell was heady and clung to their fingers, staining them dark red.

'Now roast the bread crumbs in the butter, Lucia, until they are golden brown. I shall prepare the strudel dough, it should be ready now.'

Bruno sprinkled more flour onto the marble counter and pulled gently at the dough, drawing it out to cover the counter top. 'You have to be careful with the dough, Lucia, pull gently in all directions…take care not to make any holes. Yet it must be as thin as you can get it…you should almost see through it.' The dough lay like silk fabric on the counter. 'Stroke some liquid butter over the dough…yes, with your finger…all over. Now the bread crumbs, then the cherries.

Leave a space at the end…about 10 cm and then take some sugar, rub it between your fingers and sprinkle it over the fruit.'

Lucia did as he said. The feel of the butter slipping across the fragile dough, the smell of the roasted bread crumbs, the rubbing sound of the sugar between her fingertips, how it fell like a soft snow on the cherries; plump and luscious, their juice on the verge of bursting. It all delighted her senses.

'I'll roll it up,' Bruno said. Lucia watched as he tenderly rolled the dough and teased it into a horseshoe, making sure the cherries were well spread and that the dough didn't break. He stroked some melted butter on a baking tray, brushed liquid butter on the rolled up strudel It makes it glow, he said, and popped it into a medium-high oven.

'Now Lucia, it will take 40 minutes to bake.'

'And can I taste it when it's finished?'

'Come here, Lucia.'

Lucia came to his arms and breathed in his smell. Bruno's lips caressed her cheek. 'We shall taste it when it's finished,' he said.

Lucia pressed against him as if to quiet the ripples he aroused.

'And we shall taste it while we wait.'

Dancing with Chopsticks

Yoni spread shiny slabs of sole and tuna, and slippery octopus, over the bed of gleaming ice baubles. It was hot down on the wharf and the lunchtime guests, avoiding the few seats in the sun to crowd beneath blue and white striped umbrellas, gave the old jetty bordering the fish market a bright holiday atmosphere. The unusual heat of the Spring Sydney day caressed the ice beds Yoni filled every morning. The ice would stay hard and almost untouchable well into the afternoon. But today, it was melting.

'We need more ice,' she said to Claire, her workmate at the cash register. 'I'll go and get some.'

Yoni was carting one of the ice sacks when it happened. A stab, a shot through the flesh. Electrified. The plastic sack split and she fell to the ground in a heap of tiny frozen balls. She then started to laugh and cry at the same time. She couldn't move her right arm, nor her hand. It was the hand she used her fork with, wrote with, and even though she could do enough sweet things with her left hand – like cutting rare tender meat slivers, dancing with chopsticks, arranging the lilies, orchids and irises of her ikebana creations, the loss of feeling and sensation in her right one felt as if a core part of her being had suddenly died.

In a flash, Claire was by her side. They'd met at the market and had been off for drinks once or twice. Claire sank to her knees and gently pushed Yoni's fall of black hair from her face. 'You ok?' she said softly.

Yoni looked at the freckle-faced redhead and sniffed, and then smiled. 'Guess so.'

'Try wiggling your fingers,' Claire said and stroked Yoni's cheek.

'Only the middle one works.'

'That's good enough,' said Claire. 'Come and sit in the corner out by the fig tree and I'll rub down that shoulder for you.' Claire put her arm around the slim girl with the almond-shaped eyes and drew her to her feet. Claire was half a head taller. She led Yoni over the yard to the old Moreton Bay fig whose roots formed a backrest of sorts. 'We're out of the way here. Just relax.'

Yoni smiled. She liked Claire. They were both Australian; both so different, yet both so alike.

Claire started rubbing and kneading Yoni's shoulder. 'How's the hand now?'

'Can't move more than the finger.' Yoni giggled.

'You'll have to train the other hand then,' Claire said in a soft serious voice. 'What hand do you use… to pleasure yourself?'

Yoni felt warm all of a sudden and gently spread her legs, drawing her feet up so that her knees made rounded hills over which her blue serge skirt hung like a tent. A cool breeze floated up her thighs. She tingled. 'The right one,' she whispered.

'Just a matter of getting used to it,' Claire said and kept rubbing Yoni's shoulder with her own right hand. With her left, she took Yoni's limp wrist. Claire leant over her friend, her back making a protective shield. 'I'll just spread out my skirt,' she said, and as she did so, she also loosened a button on the bodice of her white cotton blouse. 'I need room to move.'

Yoni nodded. Claire's breast was inches away from her eyes. As Claire bent to massage her shoulder she could almost taste the air around the dark skin circling Claire's taut peaking nipple. Yoni's tongue licked her lips, she could feel them swell. How she longed to suck at the breast gently swinging ripe as a mango before her. She spread her legs wider.

'Shall we see how the hand is?' Claire said softly and slipped one of her breasts from her bodice.

Yoni nodded. Her face was flushed.

Claire swallowed and then drew Yoni's hand towards the dark-haired girl's parted legs. 'I'll have to lead the way. I hope you don't mind.'

Yoni couldn't speak. She shook her head. Her pulse raced.

Claire slipped a finger in one leg of Yoni's panties and with a quick jerk pulled it down past her knees. Yoni followed invisible orders and wiggled out of the garment. Claire then took Yoni's hand in hers and guided the last conscious finger into Yoni's slit. It was wet and dripping. Claire smiled. 'It will be fine,' she said and lent in closer. Her nipple touched Yoni's lips. Yoni, needing no further invitation, lunged, closed her eyes and suckled greedily.

Claire's finger in tandem with Yoni's worked deep and deliciously in the warmth and thick wetness of Yoni's cunt. 'Is this your first time?' Claire said.

Yoni shook her head, Claire's breast still in her mouth.

'With a girl, I mean.'

Yoni suckled feverishly.

'I thought so', Claire said squatting closer. 'The poor finger needs a bit of variety,' she said and drew Yoni's hand towards her own core. The movement drew her breast from Yoni's mouth.

'It's so hot and wet,' Yoni whispered. 'And you have no panties.'

'They're not really important, are they?' Claire said. 'I mean, you didn't notice their absence. Yes, just let me guide you. Feel a difference?'

Yoni felt a warmth and a softness and then it was as if her fingers were being sucked by strong muscles and lips. Her pulse raced and she felt soaked between her own legs.

Claire's cunt was sucking, massaging her fingers. 'Your pussy is bringing my hand back to life,' Yoni said.

'Is it ever,' Claire groaned and shut her eyes.

'There is such a rich smell to what you are doing,' Yoni said dreamily now.

'I'd love to have you dance with your chopsticks, drop bits of sashimi into my cunt. I've been watching you handle those slivers of fish.' Claire was beginning to tremor.

'When my shoulder is better, I shall serve you a meal,' Yoni said. Her voice had a stroking, hypnotic quality. 'I have always done sweet things with my right hand, but you have shown me much sweeter ones to do with my left.' And with her good left hand Yoni reached forward to explore what would become her bowl for sashimi. 'I am also very good at ikebana,' she said.

'Yes. Yes, yes,' was all Claire could now say.

Culinary Foreplay

Steven Pennriahn rode across the stubbled field. The smell of freshly cut hay stacked for drying rode with him on a late summer's breeze. The harvest had been a good one and he would soon be able to enjoy the fruits of his work. He would go to France, to the town of his mother's youth. Plouescat in Brittany. Maybe he'd even find the farm she had told him about and breathe in the crisp smells of browning pancakes, paper thin and dripping with thick, full amber honey. And the Breton chants and ancient songs—perhaps he would hear them—so like the Cornish, she had told him, the Cornish that would tie the knot.

Steven arrived in Plouescat on a Tuesday in early September. The sea wind ruffled his hair and the smell of salt teased his nostrils as he walked down the narrow cobbled street to the *Auberge d'Iseult* where he had a room booked. The *Auberge d'Iseult* was a village inn built in the Breton tradition of thick, stone walls against the ocean

28

winds. It lay sheltered in a sandy bay. Steven smiled as he read the menu posted behind the glass of the tiny restaurant. It was handwritten in delicate scrawls of purple ink and told of the delights of the local fare: crepes (a pancake, paper thin, served savoury or sweet), fish and shellfish, and the vegetables of the season: cabbage, cauliflower and artichokes.

Steven's room in the Auberge was one of the small inn's two guest rooms. A cupboard was set discreetly in behind a door and a small writing table stood beneath the window looking out to sea. A vase of blue cornflowers stood on the table framed by the white cotton crochet curtains. His bed was queen-size and fluffed up with a crisp white duvet and pillows. A pity he'd have to sleep in it alone, he thought as he changed his shirt for dinner.

On his way downstairs to the restaurant of the Auberge, he turned back the cuffs of his beige linen shirt, exposing his tanned forearms. His skin had the healthy vigour of time spent outdoors and glowed golden beneath his brown freckles. His rust-coloured hair was bleached in streaks by the sun.

The dining room had five tables; each was set with crisp white linen and simple silverware. He took a seat at a table for two by the window. He was staring out to sea, watching waves lap the pebbly shore in the setting sun when he heard a warm, full voice with the whisper of a burr.

'Bonsoir, Monsieur. Vous desirez?'

Steven looked up to a smiling pair of brown eyes. He nodded slowly, then said: 'I don't speak French. Do you...?'

'Speak English?' Her eyes were laughing now. 'Yes. I do.'

She must have been in her early forties, though such things were not always easy to tell, he thought. Barest silver streaked her dark blonde hair that she wore coiled in a silky twist. Her off-white scoop necked blouse melted into a knee-length tube of velvet black.

When Steven's eyes came back to hers, she held his gaze. 'Let me recommend one of the region's specialties of the season—as an entrée.'

Steven nodded.

'Artichokes.'

'I have never eaten artichokes,' he said.

She stroked a finger around the rim of the crystal glass facing his and made it sing. 'Well then, this is the place to try...I might even show you.'

'With pleasure,' he said. 'Let me introduce myself.' He rose and held out his right hand. 'My name is Steven Pennriahn. I'm from England. Cornwall.'

'Simone Dunand,' she said and placed her small hand in his. 'This is my Auberge. *L'Auberge d'Iseult.*' Their fingers slipped away from each other and Steven sat down.

'*Iseult?*'

'The legend of Tristan and Isolde. Do you know it?'

Steven nodded slowly, thinking it over; A tragic love? A passionate one? He couldn't remember the details. The room was empty. Ash logs lay stacked neatly in the fireplace awaiting the first flames of the season. 'Will you join me, Simone?'

She looked around, then nodded. 'I have no other reservations for this evening. But first let me place your order.'

'Artichokes,' he said with a grin.

'With a creamy vinaigrette sauce?' Simone added. 'I suggest a dry local white wine. *Plannantais.*'

He cocked an eyebrow.

'Trust me,' she said.

The look in Steven's eyes signalled a nod.

'And then?' she asked as he glanced back at the menu. 'Sole?'

He nodded.

'I'll be right back,' she said, sweeping up the menu.

Steven watched her retreat. She was not tall, but her hips moved to the quiet click of her high heels across the buff country tiles in a way that brought a smile to his lips. He could have sworn that a scent of vanilla and musk lingered in the air. He closed his eyes and breathed in.

When he opened them a few seconds later, Simone was seated opposite him. She leaned forward and lit the candle in its silver candleholder.

'I've asked Pol to serve us. He has to learn,' she said with a twinkle in her eye. Steven felt a warmth prickle up his neck.

As if he had heard her words, a young blonde man came towards them with a bottle of white wine. He presented the bottle to Simone. She circled its neck with her fingers and thumb, then nodded towards Steven. Pol screwed in the opener, then drew the cork out slowly. It gave a dull pop. The young man poured a sip into Steven's glass and glanced at Simone. Steven caught her nod of approval.

The liquid glowed like ripened wheat against the candle's flame as Steven lifted his glass. He tasted its dry coolness and smiled in relief as Simone nodded at their sip of *Santé*.

Pol returned bearing two plates. A plump grey-green vegetable was poised on each like a water lily, its petals closed. He positioned a bowl of vinaigrette laced with cream on a tiny platter in the middle of the table by the silver candlestick. The orange flame flickered and three beads of red wax slithered down the candle's shaft. Steven stared down at his knife and fork. How the hell did one eat artichokes?

Simone smiled across at him. 'Use your fingers, at least at first,' she said. 'I'll show you how.' She pulled slowly on an outer leaf. 'Hold the tip. The flesh is at the base. Just dip it into the vinaigrette. Graze and scrape it ... gently…with your teeth…bring it slowly to your palate.'

Steven watched as if in trance at the way her lips and teeth enclosed the leaf. The warmth no longer prickled but flowed through him, working its way downwards.

'There's little flesh on the outside leaves. You must work your way to the heart,' she said.

Steven plucked a leaf. He shifted in his chair and placed an elbow on the table. She was right. Hardly any meat. Each leaf held enough to lead to the next and the next held more than the last. He needed both hands; one to steady the crown, the other to pluck leaf after leaf. The tang of the creamy vinaigrette soaked the flesh with a taste that tantalised with a promise of the coveted bud.

'Be careful here,' Simone said. 'You don't eat those soft fuzzy bits. They protect the heart. Just peel them off and put them aside.'

Simone plucked away the nest of soft yellow to reveal a perfect bud of pale green delicacy. It was only then that she resorted to the silver knife and fork. Her knife sank to cleave the artichoke's heart. Then she dipped her laden fork prongs into the tangy sauce.

As she paused and took a sip of wine Steven found himself gazing at the wetness glistening on her lower lip. Then she brought the fork to her lips and they closed over their booty, her lids lowering slowly to underscore the tiny sound of pleasure that escaped as she withdrew the fork. He followed suit. The flesh tanged with the sauce, its softness melted in his mouth. A sensation rippled through him far removed from culinary delight. He would never think of an artichoke as a mere vegetable again.

'Was that good? Did you like it?' Simone said as she touched her serviette to the corners of her mouth.

'Very much.' His foot touched hers under the table. 'Sorry,' he said. He wasn't.

The movement broke the spell, easing them into everyday conversation, comfortable in its blandness, yet lingering on invisible electric threads. They continued their meal of sole rolled crisply in buttery gold, sipping the cool wine. Steven spoke of his farm. He told about his mother's farm, that he had come to the region as if following a dream. She told him about her quiet life in Plouescat where she'd lived all her life. And as easily as their conversation had begun following the release of the entrée, so it ended with the sole and the promise of dessert.

'There is still work to do,' Simone said, 'but Pol shall bring yours.'

Steven cocked an eyebrow.

'Figs,' she said. 'Plump, luscious quarters laced with coffee cognac cream.' She smiled and then turned to become a dream that was perhaps now retreating from the room, but one which might even come true.

Steven dipped his finger into his wine glass then slowly circled its rim. The glass sang.

Associations

I had come home from work early. It was Valentine's Day and my lover had promised me a surprise. We were to have dinner at his place. He loved to cook, he had said, but only on special occasions. We both loved to eat. I had bought him a cookbook: *Cookbook for Lovers*. I was buzzing with excitement as I took the lift up to my sixth-floor apartment off the Boulevard Saint Michel.

I had met Alain in a small bistro when I first arrived in Paris. The restaurant was packed, but the patron seated me at the last free spot at a table for two opposite a quiet-looking man with a head of thick, dark blonde hair. There was something so unassuming about him that I didn't feel at all nervous. That came later.

I ordered *steak frites* and green salad—the usual bistro fare—and a glass of Côte du Rhone. Alain had ordered the same, but with an *entrée* of six oysters.

'Do you like oysters?' he said as the waiter placed a small plate with six open shells before him.

'I don't know,' I said.

'Would you like to taste one?'

I shook my head and he shrugged.

'They must be very fresh,' he said as he squeezed a few drops from a quarter lemon onto one of the plump pieces of flesh in its shell. The flesh quivered slightly as the juice sprinkled it. He then lifted the shell and slid the oyster into his mouth. Mesmerised by the look on his face — a moment of pure delight — I couldn't help imagining his tongue playing with this fruit of the sea before letting it slide down his throat.

'Are you sure you wouldn't like to try one?'

I shook my head. My cheeks felt hot and it was with a sense of relief that I placed a napkin on my lap when the waiter arrived with my steak.

After three weeks in Paris, I had grown more than accustomed to the rare tender meat that released a gentle trail of juice when my knife cut the flesh. I loved it. The act of eating calmed me and our conversation settled comfortably into a *getting to know you*.

We met again in the bistro. One evening we left together and he took me to his flat on the Boulevard Saint Germain. It was a simple studio; a one-room flat, with a large mattress-like divan on the honey parquet. A cluster of barley-coloured broad candles squatted in a corner by the window through which the lights of the city twinkled. Soft classical music was playing. His seduction was gentle and knowing, his caresses building a haven of trust. And so I fell in love with Alain.

We would meet in the bistro as often as possible, sometimes three, even four times a week, and here and there he would ask me again to try one of his oysters.

'They are an aphrodisiac,' he said.

'So they say.' I was not convinced.

'It all depends on associations,' he said with a wicked smile, 'and how they are made.'

I wondered about that, but when I met Alain again in the same restaurant, also by chance, he just silently ate, smiling at me between mouthfuls of *coq au vin*. We'd meet for coffee in the morning, and an *apéro* in the evening. And now it was three weeks later and a special occasion was on the menu.

I had come home early to ready myself. As I put the key in the lock, I almost stepped on a large brown envelope in front of my door. Once inside, I opened it. A gift-wrapped red paper package with hearts was inside. Smiling, I ripped it open to discover items of lingerie and a note from Alain. 'Please wear these. Til' 7 o'clock. I love you.'

My heart raced as I gingerly fingered the brassiere in dark teal blue with its trim of black lace, the matching panties, suspender belt and the sheer black stockings.

I had an hour to get ready before walking over to Alain's place so I ran a bath. A bath would relax me, I thought. And it did in a way, as I watched my breasts float like islands in the warm and fragrant water. Jasmine. Musk.

But just when my fingers strayed to play between my thighs, to slip between my nether lips and tease inside my cunt and tug and pull and tease my clit, so pleased and ready to harden, like my nipples, at the slightest ministration, I had to stop, or I would be late. And I did so want to keep my appetite, although I knew that rather than be satiated, I would only crave for more. No, I had to get ready.

I dried myself and decided against perfume. The fragrance of the bath was enough, and there was a natural fragrance I wanted to maintain. I slipped the brassiere on as I gazed at myself in the mirror. It cupped my breasts perfectly and the sheer fabric did little to hide the sudden tautness of my nipples. I fastened the belt about my waist and ran one of the sheer stockings over my hand; I slipped in my toe and peeled the fine denier slowly up to my thigh. Then I peeled on the other stocking. I gazed at myself in the mirror. Is this what he wants, I wondered. As I saw the brush of my russet pubic hair I realised that I had forgotten to put on the panties. I smiled. Alain would not dictate to me. I shall not wear them, I decided.

As I dressed—a silken black blouse and a velvet skirt that was half wrap-around to expose one leg when I walked—I began to feel more and more aroused. I wondered if it had to do with being *sans* panties for the first time in my life, or Alain's Valentine's gift. Probably both, I admitted to myself. Did I dare? Yes. I wanted to do this.

When I arrived at Alain's place, I found the door ajar so I pushed it open. Beethoven's 6th was quietly playing and there was a familiar scent of vanilla and musk.

Through the glow of a dozen large candles in the corner I saw large scarlet cushions scattered around the divan. A table for two was set in the other corner of the room. I closed the door and tiptoed to the table and then placed my cookbook gift to him on the heavy smoked glass. As I turned Alain stood before me. He was resplendent in a long midnight blue caftan. He held out his hand and drew me into his arms. Without a word, he kissed me. I had never felt so wholly ruled by my senses.

Then he spoke in a soft warm voice. 'I want to make this a special evening for you, but you must trust me.'

I raised one eyebrow, longing for more of his kisses.

'It has to do with associations,' he said. 'Are you game?'

My pulse was racing again as I felt a tiny bit moist between my legs and remembered the panties.

But Alain was already opening my blouse and pushing the front pieces away. 'Ah,' he said. 'A perfect fit.' I felt my nipples harden as he traced a finger over the fabric of the brassiere. Then his lips kissed one and then the other veiled breast. 'We shall not take it off yet,' he said. 'I want to see if the rest fits just as well.'

I didn't say a word and just stood there and waited like a nervous schoolgirl who had forgotten to do her homework. With one finger he eased the fold of my skirt aside to reveal the tops of my stockings. Then his hands slipped under my skirt and caressed their way up my thighs to the back, and as he touched the curve of my bottom I heard him give a tiny gasp before continuing as if there had been no surprise. His lips came to my ear.

'I was wondering if you would wear the panties,' he whispered. Before I could answer, he pulled at the sash that fastened the skirt and the velvet garment slid to the floor. 'Turn around,' he said and gently turned me towards a mirror against the wall.

He was standing behind me and I watched through the glowlight, hypnotised, as he slipped my blouse from my shoulders. He undid my brassiere and it fell beside the sprawled blouse on the floor. My breasts peaked firm as my heart pounded. I didn't dare move, caught in some sublime trance.

Alain's hands circled my midriff and gently explored beneath the suspender belt. I was tingling. Then his fingers dipped into my russet hairs and I was forced to close my eyes. I was so wet and I knew that he would soon feel the moisture about to trickle down the inside of my thighs. He did, and I opened my eyes.

With one finger, as if skimming a delectable topping, he grazed the soft pulsing flesh, now swollen under his ministrations, and brought it to his nostrils as if to breathe in the scent of a rare and precious wine.

'I can smell that you are game,' he said as he led me to the divan and gently laid me down on my back. 'There is no need for you to do anything, my love. Tonight is your night,' he whispered and peeled off my stockings and unfastened the last garment. All the while, he still wore his caftan, a tell-tale sheen now shining through below his waistline.

I closed my eyes. Beethoven was still playing, but there was a new urgency to its allegro as Alain began stroking my breasts and suckling my nipples, caressing my hips and the insides of my thighs; he avoided the source of my juices in a way that tantalized, until inspired, a sudden clutch from within me.

He then took my hand and placed it at the top of the inside of my right thigh.

'Can you wait for me a moment like this?'

I sighed and closed my eyes, enveloped in a heaven of senses, but left longing for more. It seemed as if my body had taken on a life of its own in a new world of sensations. My fingers began to explore the swollen lips between my legs, dipping deeper into what I thought must be nectar, so thick it felt.

The nub of my clit was taut and throbbing, my fingers didn't stop moving and then suddenly Alain's soft voice eased through my moans. 'Hush now my darling, but keep your eyes closed.'

I was torn between action and anticipation. My heart was thumping almost louder than Beethoven.

'Breathe deeply, slowly,' Alain said. I did. As I began to calm down, his fingers eased their way into my pussy, displacing mine. Cool, they stroked the flesh of my swollen nub and then…the tremor of a new sensation of liquid, soft, gentle cold, giving way to a myriad of tiny clutches. My fingers, still wet, tugged at my nipples, twisting and tugging, them until I felt a warmth, a deep sucking, a soft caressing, a probing, all at the same time.

Heat and cool fused and I thought my core must explode, carrying me beyond all living memory, and then subsiding to feel a gentle nibbling of my throbbing clit.

Alain stroked my belly and drew his head up. As his warm moist lips kissed mine I felt as if I must drown in the love of him and the appealing new taste.

'Is that me?' I whispered.

He gently nuzzled my neck. 'You,' he said, 'and oyster. Would you like to try one now?' He smiled at me and his finger swirled inside me, squeezing, pushing a plump softness until my cunt felt it was drowning in a liquid thickness. My voice was hoarse as I whispered, 'Oyster?'

'My usual appetizer,' he said. 'But on this special occasion, I'd like to attend some more to a marinade.' He rolled the 'r' with a low growl.

It was then I saw the silver plate. Six open shells. Two empty. Alain slipped a second finger into what had now become a receptacle of precious juices. I couldn't help stretching my legs wider apart.

'Wider,' he said and pushed my fingers into my cunt. 'Keep twirling, swirling.' He took a shell and held it beneath my nose. I closed my eyes. The rough shell scraped my swollen labial lips. My fingers worked the juices.

'Please,' I moaned.

'So you would like to try?' he said as the fleshy mollusc slipped inside me. I gasped. My fingers were now toiling furiously. 'You must beat more than that, *mon amour*. Come, I shall help you.'

There was no holding back. 'Let me taste,' I groaned. 'Let me, let me…'

'Just the last two. One stays there to warm a little. The other is for you.' And he slipped two more oysters into my overflowing pussy. The last one he swirled about in the marinade and then scooped it to my lips. I put my head back, my mouth was open. 'Let me,' I groaned.

At last he slipped the oyster into my mouth. I caught it with my tongue, probed, until the thick liquid burst the fragile membrane and filled my mouth; slowly I swallowed the spent mollusc, heady almost as it slid down my throat. My breathing slowed and then a sudden final clutch spread a glow, a relaxation, a final coming as Alain hungrily slurped the remains of his appetizer from its more than satisfied receptacle.

He moved his head, his swollen satiated mouth, over my belly, my midriff to reach my breasts and suckled gently, a trail of cunt and oyster nectar gleaming on my skin. He held me close in his arms for a time which seemed without measure, then got up and handed me an emerald silk caftan that must have been tucked behind one of the cushions.

'Please wear this,' he said. 'It goes so beautifully with your hair.'

The silk rustled and caressed my body as I slipped on the caftan. I was speechless with wonder and with hunger.

'Shall we eat now?' Alain said and held out his hand to lead me to the table. I leaned into him and held him close. 'I have a side dish of asparagus,' he said softly, 'and then some tender, succulent beef.'

Alain knew how I loved asparagus, and beef, and I knew that my cookbook gift was filled with recipes for many special occasions. And my new love of oysters, I knew, I would always associate with Alain.

Mushroom Strudel

Simone left her Renault behind Steven's Jeep and ran to the front door of the cottage. She pulled the fur-trim of her hooded parka close around her cheeks, thumped the brass horse-head knocker and waited. She thumped again. Wiggling the round knob, Simone found the door unlocked. She pushed it open. A slapping sound came from the kitchen. She edged closer.

A young woman in an oversized sweat shirt and large woollen socks stood with her back to Simone. The girl was engrossed in slapping a white mass onto a marble slab and kneading it. Dark red curls tumbled over her shoulders. Her hips rolled as she dipped to her knees, baring a décolleté of buttocks beneath French silk panties.

Simone cleared her throat. The girl spun around. Green eyes looked Simone up and down. Simone felt a prickly warmth creep up her neck. Who was this girl? Where was Steven? What was she doing here in Steven's clothes?

'Bonjour,' said Lucia.

'I was looking for Steven, the Englishman. Are you ... a friend?'

'You could say that. My name's Lucia. You must be Simone.'

Simone froze. 'How do you know? Where is he?'

Lucia turned back to the table, took up the white mass of dough and slapped it once again onto the marble slab. 'He went to chop wood,' she said. 'He was out all morning ... picking mushrooms.'

Simone's eyes fell on the rough wicker basket heaped with autumn's spoils: golden chanterelle, translucent grey oyster mushrooms, black wizened morels and the creamy-tawn king *bolete* with its pale spongy underside.

'You have to be careful,' she said. Lucia kept kneading. 'I told Steven which ones were poisonous. There were some he didn't know.'

There was something disturbing about the young woman. Simone felt her cheeks warm like a pre-heating oven, baking emotions of jealousy, sadness and seduction like forest scents or fresh, yeasty dough. Simone slipped off her parka and hung it over the back of a chair.

'I'm making Strudel,' Lucia said. 'Mushrooms. Wild ones. Although I shall mix in the *shiikate*.' She turned her green eyes on Simone. 'Don't you think they'd give it an exotic touch?'

Simone fingered the mushrooms in the basket. She glanced at Lucia bearing down on the dough. 'Do you want me to help…clean them?'

Lucia nodded. 'Take that apron over there.' She stopped, both hands resting on the dough. 'The oven's heating. Don't you want to take off your pullover?' she said, her eyes travelling over Simone's ochre mohair.

Simone pulled off the mohair and attached the apron, slipping the fastened bib over her head. The apron skirt dipped down to protect her front.

'Perhaps knead the dough. It's quite tiring,' Lucia said and sprinkled more flour on the counter. 'So that it won't slip,' she added and pushed a strand of hair from her forehead with the back of her hand, causing tiny speckles of flour to trace her jawbone.

Simone wiped her hands on her apron and plunged both hands into the dough.

'Push down, Simone. Push with both heels of your hands. Draw the dough back with your fingers. Keep the rhythm.'

Simone pulled and pushed, and pulled and pushed. Her whole body was moving in harmony. As she leant forward to push with the heels of her hands across the counter, her knees bent so slightly in a rolling motion that swelled through to her shoulders bearing down on the dough.

Lucia took a step back to gaze at the hypnotic movement. The only sound was the cool flap-flap against the marble and the sound of rhythmic breathing. Simone kept on kneading, eyes half closed.

'That's good,' Lucia said and began cutting earth and rough edges from the mushrooms.

The pearly dough felt like silk in Simone's hands. She bore down, kneading, building up a gentle rhythm. It had a strangely calming effect, yet gave way to a prickling about her chest. As she loosened the buttons of her moss green silk blouse, her eyes met Lucia's.

The younger woman held the creamy crown of the king *bolete* and was plucking away the fleshy stem. She ran her fingers over the sponge almost as if in a caress. 'It's so soft, so fragile,' she murmured, 'yet so resistant.'

Simone felt a triggering in her core and lowered her eyes to concentrate on the dough.

'Ever done this before?' Lucia asked.

Simone looked at Lucia. Her throat blocked the sound of her voice as she slowly shook her head.

'Mushroom strudel... I mean,' Lucia said. Her green eyes laughed.

So she's calling my bluff, Simone thought. The strange thing was that it had become a game, and each layer of apprehension was slowly being stripped away. No longer jealous, Simone found she was becoming the object of Lucia's desire. It was an unusual and new feeling, even if it felt like being equated to the insides of a mushroom. Simone laughed.

Lucia looked up, puzzled. 'May I share?' she asked.

'Seems to be what it's all about,' she said. 'The king *bolete* certainly is a magnificent specimen.'

Lucia pulled off her sweatshirt and stretched her arms. 'It's getting hot,' she said.

'Indeed,' Simone said with a smile.

Lucia looked down at her oversized socks and giggled. Her silk camisole top barely hid the tautness of her nipples. Simone felt a gentle wave push through her at the sight of Lucia's arousal. How was this game to be played? she thought. Just let the wave carry you, a voice inside her whispered.

Then Lucia came round to Simone's side of the table. 'Aren't you hot? We're all alone here, you know. Just us girls.' She smiled as she slipped the tape of the apron over Simone's neck and let the bib dip down to her knees. Simone closed her eyes as Lucia's fingers slipped each pearly button of her blouse through each snug buttonhole. Her breasts ached for attention as tiny ripples ran within her.

'You're lovely, Simone,' Lucia whispered behind her ear and gently teased a finger about one nipple. It hardened instantly.

Simone's pulse raced. She didn't move, almost swaying in a trance to the stroking of Lucia's finger.

'There, that's better,' Lucia said as she slipped the blouse from Simone's arms. Then she brought the bib back over Simone's head. 'Want me to handle the dough a while?'

Simone nodded. She glided to the other side of the table. The mushrooms were soft and pliant under her fingers. She cut through them easily with the sharp knife, like cutting through room-warm butter.

'I've already chopped the leeks, the *shiikate* and the walnuts,' Lucia said. 'Just mix them in and add the oregano, sesame seeds and pepper ... as you would in your own kitchen,' she added with the hint of a smile.

Simone's fingers sifted through the browns and beiges and ambers, revelling in the change of textures from the soft and moist of the mushrooms and leeks to the hard, smooth feel of the walnuts. She added a generous dollop of soy sauce and mixed in some cooked rice, breathing in the precious aromas released by her ministrations.

Lucia rolled out the dough. 'It has to be very thin,' she said. 'Almost see-through, like the silk of your blouse.' One strap of her camisole had slipped from her shoulder. 'We can spread the mushrooms. Come. Help me roll the strudel.'

Simone carried the bowl of sliced mushrooms back to Lucia's side. A rich scent rose to her nostrils, an exciting blend of fresh dough, forest musk and a hint of jasmine. She could hold back no longer. She placed the bowl on the table and her lips caressed Lucia's shoulder. Gingerly she slipped a finger under the strap of the camisole bringing it back up Lucia's arm. Her hand brushed Lucia's nipples peaking through the sheer fabric. All she could hear was a faint swishing of silk and the beating of her own heart. With both hands Simone pushed up the camisole and buried her face in Lucia's breasts. Lucia sighed and caressed Simone's head. 'It has to bake for 40 minutes,' Lucia said. 'Let's finish the strudel first.'

Simone drew back flushed. She watched Lucia expertly roll the mushrooms in the dough and place the horseshoe shape on a tray. With a brush she stroked melted butter over the top. 'To make it glow,' she said. Then she popped the strudel in the oven. Wiping her hands on Simone's apron, she said: 'Do you trust me, Simone?'

They were breast to breast. Simone searched Lucia's face. 'Yes,' she said simply. This young woman had opened up new sensations, ones she had never known. She was introducing her to new delights, recapturing a youth she had let slip away. How could she not trust her? 'Yes,' she said, 'I trust you, Lucia.'

'Then turn around.'

Simone turned, obeying as if in a trance.

From out of nowhere, Lucia slipped a black satin sash over Simone's eyes and tied a bow at the back of her head. Simone saw nothing, yet her senses were heightened. The scents of the forest, of rising yeast, of baking warmth, enveloped her. She heard the gentle dribbling of the tap in the sink, the swishing of movements. Lucia's? Was she leaving. Simone's heart raced again. She couldn't leave. Trust her. Trust her.

'I'm here, Simone,' Lucia said. 'Imagine. Just imagine a winter's warm dessert, the smell of nutmeg, cinnamon ...'

Simone closed her eyes beneath the sash. She could feel the warm tingle of cinnamon as a warmth rose around her. The back of a strong, gentle hand stroked her cheek. As firm fingers slipped down the side of her neck over her chest and large warm hands cupped her breasts, she smiled and stretched her hands out to feel lean, naked masculine hips beneath her palms.

Slowly she moved her palms to each other, her fingers outstretched, feeling the tight mound of an abdomen; the heels of her palms grazed coarse springy hairs and as her thumbs came together something strong, soft and alive nudged them away. Simone slid to her knees and took Steven's strength, knowing she must drown in the nutmeg taste of him.

By the Skin of the Nose

My name is Scaramouche. I'm a private dick. No, it's not what you think. It never is. My brief was to traipse my taste buds over your body's largest organ. The skin. It never is what you think. Did you know that taste is a cop out? There's only so much diversity in a lick. And anyway, 80% of taste is in the nose: smell, fragrance, odour, pong, stench, scent, the blind man's *senso di donna* ...now I'm warming to the task. Come here. Slip out of those clothes. Pass each item to me. Yes, I know that this is about skin, but haven't you heard of foreplay? Get those smell sensors twitching now. No, smell isn't about shape; that would leave so much in the dark and anyway I go for all shapes and sizes. Smell's about vibrations. Good ones. Come with me now on an olfactory tour. Close your eyes, keep your gloves on and let me sniff the geography of your body. Let me wander my schnozzle up hill and down dale, into valleys of mangroves where rainforests seep out to the ocean.

The skin around the toes is an acquired taste, a little like a fine rotting cheese from a small town in Germany. But rub in a pat of butter and you can easily slip through each of the crevices onto that finest of mica sheathing the foot. Let me rub my nose into traces of Blahnik. I can smell that tights clothed your legs; nylon has a way of leaving a clingy aroma of warmed-up winter. Let me go to your hands now. Your palm smells salty, and where have you been with those fingers? Impatient one, Oyster Girl, or do I discern the sweet pong of a puckering butthole? My nose roams the length of your arms and burrows your armpits *au naturel*. Sweet sweaty stench of pre-copulation. Breathe in for me.

The back of your neck is cool and welcomes me to the warm peach scent of your hair. I rest there a while before slipping between your breasts to sniff at a hint of milky warm flesh in the creases. May I turn you over now? Just to prolong matters? My nostrils follow that bead of perspiration running between those two dimples and on down to your buttocks. You raise them and I sniff down your crack, breathing in the full strength of your sweet fecal smell. It's making me dizzy. Turn now. Let me burrow my nose into the warm wet folds of your cunt. I dive, breathing in, and drown as their silken sweet urgency fills my nostrils. And that's when I start lapping it all up.

Soul Kill

Marja stands at the lights and waits for the little green man to spread his legs. She dips a hand into the pocket of her skirt and fingers her passport. What choice does she have? All that is left now is an expired visa. She shivers in the clammy night air and crosses over.

Marja stops at the house in full view of the traffic. Its raised door is tiled with mirrors. She stares at the peephole in the middle of her forehead and in her reflection sees Jakub's face. 'Get out of my head,' she says aloud.

'Got a place to stay?' he'd asked on her first day in Sydney as she pulled her carry-all down Central Station. His accent she'd recognised as New Europe. Why not, she thought, it somehow fitted into her new world. Jakub was from Prague and had been in Australia for six months. A plumber with golden hands, he'd slipped in as a migrant in response to loud calls for young able workers. 'It was easy,' he said. 'I have the right skills.'

They made love the first night. 'You can stay here,' he'd said. 'And when I run out of money?' Marja'd asked with a laugh. 'Then I'll sell your body,' he said. 'You wouldn't dare,' she said. 'No,' he'd said as he tucked her gently into his doona.

Marja runs a hand through her hair as if to free herself from his face in her reflection. She presses the button and the door opens; the evening traffic drowns in a fug.

'I have an appointment,' Marja says. A nerve twitches on the left side of her neck as she adjusts to the dim light that makes her blouse bone white in the walls of mirrors.

'Is this your first time?' a tall sullen man asks.

Marja's hands are dry but her left palm is damp. 'You mean professionally?' she says.

The man nods.

'I have to start somewhere,' she says. 'But I want to be safe.' She'd felt so safe with Jakub. He'd promised she wouldn't have to go back to Poland, that he'd make it all legal, a fresh start in his life.

The tall sullen man leads her down a deep stairway and she catches a whiff of a sweet yeasty scent. How safe is safe, she wonders. It was all relative now.

At the end of the corridor the man opens a door. Rough stones frame mirrors along a black wall. Gleaming chains hang from the ceiling; others dangle from padded braces. A pillory, its head and wrist holes painted in silver, stands by an embedded shower. Marja smells the faint odour of bath liquid. It was the same brand Jakub had in his bathroom. He'd taken her under the shower, his hands and lips slippering over her body. Get out of my head, she whispers.

'Strip,' says the tall sullen man. 'Let's see what you've got.'

Marja undresses and kicks her clothes aside. The man's eyes graze on her body while she tries to ignore the twitch at her throat. It had twitched the same way when Jakub had peeled the clothes from her body. But the tiles are cold here under her bare feet.

The tall sullen man takes a black silk scarf from his pocket and trails it over her shoulder and collarbone. As the edging runs over her breasts she feels a tiny clutch deep below her gut. Jakub had known all about the clutch. 'How does it feel?' he'd asked softly. Please get out of my head.

'Do you like cats?' the tall sullen man asks.

Marja swallows. She closes her eyes and feels Jakub nuzzle her. 'I know why it's called pussy,' he'd said, and she'd giggled. She opens her eyes. Jakub is gone. Please stay away.

The tall sullen man takes a whip from the wall: it is long and black and has five plaited tails. 'Hold out your hand and close your eyes,' he says.

The twitch at her throat is going wild. Marja holds out her open palm and feels the tails trail over her lifeline, her shoulders, her breasts, down her stomach. Then they stop an instant to start again at her feet, moving upwards on the inside of her calves, making her thighs part almost instinctively. She feels the clutch, a small hand grabbing at her core. Jakub, she breathes. She is wet.

The tall sullen man shackles her wrists to the chains from the ceiling. Then he ties the silk scarf over her eyes. Marja grasps at the chains. The cat strokes her back and she lets herself sway. Then it snaps on her buttocks and her eyes rip open, see the black of the scarf and Jakub's silky hair. He is with her now. The cat strokes again and she relaxes. Then it flicks the insides of her thighs and she smells the warm fragrance of her own arousal. 'Don't stop,' she says.

'That's what you need to hear in this business,' says the tall sullen man as he unclasps her chains and unties the scarf. Marja's throat pulses openly now. 'It's just the beginning,' he adds and slips a folded twenty note between her thighs. Marja clamps her legs to steady herself.

The tall sullen man scoops up her bra and panties and stuffs them into his pocket. 'Get dressed,' he says. 'In five minutes you're on. The one in the green suit.'

'How much?' she asks flatly.

'He pays upstairs first and he'll give you eighty,' he says, and then adds: 'You just got twenty.'

'Open your life,' Tina Turner sings as the middle-aged man takes off his green suit and hangs it neatly over the pillory. He stands naked with just socks and shoes on. His penis is flaccid.

Marja stares at his socks. Jakub had kept his socks on. 'Can't say I was always in bed with you naked,' he'd said and then kissed her. Be gone now, please.

'You'll have to guide me a little,' she says. Her hand reaches unsteadily for the five-tailed cat and grazes the puckered rash of the wall.

'Shackle me first,' the man says. 'Unbutton your blouse, but close your collar.' He grabs the chains and hangs back.

'The cat now?' Marja asks. Please finish this thing. Get it over.

'Not yet,' says the man. 'Just look at me and fondle your breasts. Take the cat to me when you see me stiffen.'

Marja pulls the tails of the cat through her hand and flicks the ends over her breasts. The man's penis salutes. He can't wait, she thinks and slashes the soft tails across his chest. Let him come hard and let it be soon, she prays.

The man's eyes are begging as Marja trails the cat with firm flicks down his arms to his waist. His penis swells. 'The cock,' he pleads.

'A little tight, is it?' Let him come hard. No seconds, please.

'The foreskin.'

Marja moves closer and rubs against him.

'Pull it back,' he says.

'That'll leave you in limbo,' she says and spits into her hand. There is something pitiful about the man. A salsa beat pulses up. 'Like this?' she says as she envelopes his penis and eases him free.

The man nods. 'The cat,' he says hoarsely.

Marja flicks the man's cock with her whip. He closes his eyes and hangs open mouthed. Part of her is repulsed, but another part admires his courage. She expected a deep silence of groans and dirty talking, but the man has spelled out his needs. He at least knows them, she thinks as she raises her arm and slashes the tails through the air.

And what are my needs in this new world? Her visa was up. The day before she was due to leave, Jakub had gone out for cigarettes. She'd waited and waited. She'd filled the waiting with smoking the butts of Jakub's joints, drinking the dredges in his collection of bottles until sleep claimed her. When she awoke she turned on the TV and spent what seemed a slow-motion lifetime staring at the buzz on the screen before she fled. Alone now. Illegal. She needed money to live; for how long, and for what?

Marja brushes her hair. The man is now dressed in his green suit. She straightens his bowtie and he tucks a crisp hundred into her belt.

'You get change,' Marja says and pulls the twenty from her waistband.

The man sniffs like a dog and grabs the damp note. 'Next time I'll bring you a fresh one,' he says. Techno pounds and Marja feels that her eardrums must burst.

As Marja comes out, the traffic revs up and the lights turn red. 'I will sell your body,' she hears Jakub say. 'Don't you dare,' she whispers and fronts up to the kerb. 'No,' he says. 'Yes,' she replies and steps out of her shoes and onto the street, dodging the cars to the blaring of horns.

Vichyssoise

When I was young I loved older men. They gave me gifts and taught me a lot. A lot about balls and sucking cock. And a lot about cooking.

As time went by I developed a penchant for younger men. They let me take the lead and I had them in the palm of my hand, in a manner of speaking. I taught them a little about what pussy liked, and they loved my recipes.

I still enjoyed men, but as I got older I began craving something quite different. My new lover is a vibrant executive and is precociously adept at beating men at their game. Much younger than I, my lover is charming, bright, and adores my recipes. She also has a soft spot for pearls, one of the first things I noticed the day we met in a supermarket downtown.

She was after one of those ready-made salads and was leaning across the herbs, blocking my view of the dill and the basil, but exposing the freshest breast with the tightest of brown nipples. Creamy pearls swayed from the slant of her grey power suit, no doubt teasing those nubs to the shape of arousal. Never had a woman's breast moved me, at least never like that, all the way down.

'Have you seen the chives?' I said.

She turned. The movement suddenly pulled me within that unspoken ring of heightened interest, crossing the border from decorum to intimacy. My throat felt hot. It wasn't the first time. It had been happening often lately, but not quite like this. She spun around, back to me, and then turned, a bunch of chives in her hand, held out like a bouquet.

The movement took me by surprise. Bold, it brought me back to the present. 'Thank you,' I said and then smiled.

'What are you making?'

'It's for Vichyssoise.'

'Vichyssoise? You can make that yourself?'

I nodded.

'I'd love to try some.'

And I'd love you to do that, I thought. But we were in a supermarket and I didn't know her name.

'My name's Sam. Short for Samantha,' she said.

What could I do but answer. 'Sophia,' I said. And then we shook hands.

I don't know if was because of the way her hand lingered in mine. Her hand was soft and warm yet felt so strong and then it seemed as if the touch of our hands somehow sealed a sensual pact; and it all seemed so natural. So I invited Sam to come home and watch me prepare the cold soup.

I lost little time in readying the ingredients for the Vichyssoise: the white delicate parts of leek, washed well and slivered; the potatoes peeled and sliced thin; the butter, melted evenly over a low, low heat that swallowed the leeks which turned gradually golden. The aroma was comforting, almost homey. 'Would you like some wine?' I said.

Sam nodded. 'Do you mind if I slip off my shoes?'

I poured two glasses from an open bottle of St Émilion. 'You can slip out of that jacket as well if you like. I'll get you a cardigan.'

Sam sipped her wine. 'I'd like that,' she said.

When I came back with the apricot cashmere, Sam stood with her back to me, 'sans' jacket and stirring the leeks in the butter. 'Thank you for keeping an eye on the soup,' I said.

Sam suddenly turned, the wooden spoon in her right hand. The baroque pearls hung over one breast, just grazing the nipple.

'They're gorgeous,' I whispered.

A thick droplet of soup rolled from the spoon.

'Careful,' I said as I took the spoon from her hand and laid it down gently in the porcelain spoon rest.

'Slip into this.'

I handed her my favourite cardigan and watched her dress.

She began to button two holes at her midriff and I found myself praying that she would not button much higher. As if reading my mind she just buttoned one more.

'Do we add the potatoes?' she asked.

My cheeks felt hot. 'We have to add chicken stock first, then we slip in the potato slivers.'

'I can do it,' she said and leant by my arm, affording me a full view of both delicious breasts as she gently shook the potato slices into the unctuous mixture. When it had simmered to a soft texture, I showed her how to puree, pushing, kneading with an antique masher, a gift from a former culinary lover. When the texture was fine we added milk and pepper and simmered again.

'It smells so good,' Sam said.

'Cold soups like to be over-seasoned,' I said. 'They can take it.'

Then we added the cream: I poured as Sam stirred, swirling the cream gently into a soup that before my eyes was metamorphosing from a hearty peasant stock to a luxurious sop of bourgeois decadence. The whole process was starting to transport me from simple arousal to an exciting state of pre-orgasm.

'What about the chives?' Sam said.

Her voice brought me back. I had arranged the chives in a glass. 'They'll be chopped and sprinkled all over.'

'I want to taste it,' she said.

I shook my head. 'You'll have to wait.'

'Please?'

'It has to chill overnight.' I was enjoying being in charge. It was something I relished, even if just once in a while.

'I can't wait,' she said. 'Unfortunately.' And then she stroked a finger down my cheek, past my throat and suddenly slipped her hand in my bra and pinched my already taut right nipple. Then, as if a question she had asked had just been answered, she withdrew her hand, cupped my face in her palms and kissed me fully on the lips. Her tongue darted between them. 'Can I visit you when I am back in town?' she whispered.

'When will that be?' My voice was hoarse.

'Two weeks. Can I borrow the cardigan?'

I nodded. I had tried hard, but again I was smitten. She loved my food. It always was the way to my core.

Sam comes back regularly. She doesn't have much time, but what she does have is pure quality. Intense. Good to look forward to. It lets me consolidate, take stock. It's better for her and for me. For her, as it lets her get on with her work and lets her get off as she chooses. And for me. I can play with my cooking, indulge my memories and fantasies and look forward to her coming.

Sam brings me gifts when she comes every few weeks. Fragrant oils: vanilla, musk. Sometimes toys, to keep me going until her next visit. Once she brought me a couple of shiny shocking pink balls connected by a pink latex string. A tiny looped stringlet for hooking a finger to ease the balls out hung cheekily from one of them; I couldn't resist fingering it for size.

'Wear them for a few hours daily,' Sam said. 'They will tone your muscles.'

I did. They were smooth, fitted snugly inside me. Because they were weighted and the little weights moved when I did, I swore that my shocking pink balls also sang. My cunt sang as I walked and I thrilled to the thought that others might hear. I'd walk at home naked and with slow rhythmic movements I'd expose my ripe cunt lips and sweet puckered butthole to the glint of glass in the sunlight coming from a window across the way. I'd sometimes sit facing the long French windows and thrill to the thought of the show I was giving as I twirled and tugged on the string of my balls, rocking my hips and listening to the soft twang.

But that and another sensation were ones I kept to myself: I didn't tell Sam about the added value of my clit nub fitting just into the little loop handle so that when I walked and rolled my hips to the tune of a rhythmic twang, the tiny girdle would keep me going. and more importantly, coming. It was quite delectable as she was to see when she withdrew the balls on her next visit. They were covered in cream.

'Mmm, reminds me of something,' she said, as she took each ball in her mouth. 'I never did get to taste the chilled soup.'

'I poured in some cream at the end. Brought it almost to body temperature.'

'I've missed you. Wear your pink balls to dinner.'

I wanted nothing better than that. I was empty and nicely throbbing and longed to be filled again, especially with her there. It was summer time. Thick creamy, cold soup with a smattering of chives would be just the thing. The bistro down the street was open and served Vichyssoise.

At dinner we sat side by side and as we were about to sip from our wine she asked me: 'Are you wearing your balls?' I smiled and then nodded. 'Good,' she said. 'And I have a new gift.' Sam passed me a little cloth bag. Grey pearl earrings. Perfectly baroque. I pierced them through my lobes and Sam stuck her tongue in my ear, swirling it around to finish with a lap over the dark pearly nub.

We walked the two blocks back to my apartment. I could hear the subtle ding of the pink balls within me. Sam had a hand down the back of my pants and was caressing my crack. 'Stick your butt out a bit as you walk,' she whispered and licked my earlobe, sucking imperceptibly on my pearl. I did as I was told; the balls inside me moved deliciously, and as I tensed my muscles the little girdle pulled on my clitoris. Her middle finger was stroking the puckered skin of my arse. I loved the sensation, but I was not going to come in the middle of the street. That would be going too far, far too soon. 'Sam!'

Sam withdrew her hand and laughed. 'I have something else,' she said. 'But wait till we're comfortable.'

Out on the balcony in the moonlight she undressed me. I wondered if my neighbour was watching. Although I couldn't see the glint of his telescope by night, I knew he was in for another show. Or was it a she? A friend of

Sam's maybe? Checking on me? I laughed. I loved the idea of somebody watching.

'Lie down,' Sam said. I did as was told. She played with my nipples and then, as if she couldn't wait any longer, her hand slipped between my thighs and her finger hooked in the little clit girdle. 'That's enough now. It's my turn. Hold your breath.' She pulled gently and one ball popped out, sulkily almost, and then the other.

I was throbbing. 'I'm so wet, Sam.'

'I can see that.'

The balls were dripping. 'It's much thicker this time.'

'*Crème de la crème*. Hotter than Vichyssoise, my darling. Come suck with me,' she said. And we each sucked my cream from both of the balls.

'I said I had something special. Close your eyes and lean back,' Sam said.

Again, I did as told. Suddenly, I felt a delicious cold, caviar like, hard as pearls, but a little irregular. She crammed them into my cunt. The sensation of the shapes and the cold was mind-blowing.

'Open your eyes.'

She held a mirror in front of me. Two diamond clasps at the end of a string of pearls the size of hazelnuts hung from my pussy. She pushed and rubbed.

'How does that feel?'

I was exploding. Lights shooting behind my eyes. Creaming.

'You look gorgeous like that. I knew we'd find a special way to share my Tahitian pearls.' Then she pulled them slowly from my cunt, each one rubbing the insides of my vagina, running over my clit, against my swollen lips, bringing with the pearls a gush from the sea within me. I had never experienced anything like it. 'Sam, I'm ...'

'Ejaculating,' she said triumphantly. 'Join the club, darling.' Then she pulled down her pants and straddled my face. 'Suck me dry, baby.'

'You know that's impossible, Sam,' I said as I burrowed my face between her thighs and began lapping the flow of her thick warm juices.

'Remind you of something?'

'Mmmm,' I said. The cream always comes right at the end, but I swear I could taste a slight tang of chives.

Mangrove on Wenceslas Square

Magda stares down at the street through parted lace curtains. Two trams have already rattled towards Mala Strana and the figure is still there as if etched on the backdrop of time-battered houses.

Magda touches her throat and the lace curtain flutters. Her fingers dip to the slight rise of her breasts and rest there in a vain move to calm her breathing. It is Romina. Magda wonders why she has returned. She pulls back the curtain. The figure looks up and their eyes lock.

Romina. Twenty years was a long time, but people had waited longer than that. The figure pulls at the hood of her tan duffle coat and crosses the street. Magda hears the light skip of footfall on the stone stairs up to her flat, just a stone's throw from Prague Castle. Then she shared the flat with Jiři; Now she is alone.

She quickly draws the curtains and unconsciously strokes her thighs, sensing rather than feeling the velvet of her long dressing gown.

She had stroked her thighs the same way so long ago, and so seldom since that day she had lingered in the hallway. Jiři had been dead now for almost twenty years. Yet Romina had come back.

***

'This is Romina. She's from Australia,' Jiři had said as he laughingly pushed the young woman before him.

'That's far away,' Magda said, holding her hand out. 'Welcome.'

Romina shook it and smiled. 'Thank you.'

'I want to make love to her, Magda.'

'You are drunk,' Magda said.

'Yes.' And he swung around with Romina in his arms, her long dark hair fanning out as they twirled.

'We didn't have that much Pils,' Romina said, laughing.

'I'm drunk on you,' Jiři said.

'I'll get something to eat,' Magda said and reached for her coat from the hook in the hall. 'Don't worry. I'll take my time,' she added, her voice fading.

'Thanks, …' and turning to Romina, Jiři said, 'What is it you say in Australia? Mate?'

Romina nodded.

'Thanks, mate.'

Mate, Magda thought, her face now flushing. Her mate for the soul, sometimes for the body. But for Magda that had been good enough. She no longer needed to fight back any tears. Habit had taught her just to accept. Would there ever be room for hopes and for dreams?

She slipped into her coat and from a drawer in the small wooden kitchen table plucked a string bag to carry the sausage and bread she would buy. As she left, she heard Romina's voice humming strange words: beaches and bush; rainforests soaking into mangrove swamps, thinning into the ocean. That would just be Jiří's type of freedom. Magda tossed her blonde head and ran down the stairs chanting a list in her mind: butter, bread, wine, *kolbasa*.

Magda crossed the Charles Bridge with its statues, stopping to rub the brass plaque, shiny from so many hands and so many hopes. Jiří was so easily enflamed, for a cause, for a woman. But her acceptance was stronger than any jealous ache. She had to accept. Jiří's flame was the cause; fuelled by the slightest promise of freedom it lapped at her heart. It wasn't just women. Politics too. Did he really think Dubček would bring a new Spring? This Australian girl was nothing but another fresh breath soon to be consumed like all the others before her. And it would be Magda who prevailed in the end.

Her shopping done, Magda slowly climbed the three floors to the flat. She pushed open the door and emptied the bag on the kitchen table. She took off her coat, hung it on the hook by the glass door to the flat's one big room and suddenly paused. She could not help seeing through the lace covering the door pane.

The mattresses that doubled as couches between books piled to the ceiling were now in the centre of the room. Romina faced her, straddling Jiři. The young woman's hair fell like black satin sheets from her shoulders. Her full breasts swung teasingly in Jiři's face. One breast was caught.

'Suck harder... Yes.' She pulled back and swung her body slowly, as if she were screwing herself into Jiři, round and round, deeper and deeper.

Magda could not look away. Her hand came to her throat and her fingers came to rest on a quickening rising in her breast. Romina threw back her head and it was if her thick sheets of hair held her contorted, her breasts upthrust, her nipples tender, so tender, from so much suckling. Magda cupped her own breast and sought her own now taut nipple. She tweaked slowly, then quickened the pressure. Romina swung upright and her eyes locked with Magda's through the lace curtain. A painfully delicious clutch invaded that place between Magda's hungry thighs, forcing her to confront Romina's questioning gaze. The moment seemed like forever, then suddenly stopped.

Magda breathed slowly, her hands slightly trembling, as she sliced the sausage and bread. She concentrated on cutting the thinnest of slices, smearing them with butter; slicing the hard dark sausage; spreading the slices on each piece of black rye. Her hands calm, she took down three glasses and placed them on an old silver tray with a bottle of red wine. Bearing the tray, she pushed the door open. Jiři must have just had time to zip up his jeans. Romina sat demurely on the edge of one mattress now moved back to its place by the wall. So this was the rainforest meeting the ocean.

The next day the tanks came. People rushed out to the broad avenue leading up to Wenceslas Square. Some were beaten back by policemen, khaki-clad figures in white shiny helmets. Others assembled, their lines haphazard like the gravestones of the Jewish cemetery: just flesh against metal. Jiři was in the front line as the tanks ploughed through the bodies. As if in trance the women witnessed the scene. Magda was the first to react. 'You must go,' she said to Romina. 'Quickly. For your own sake.'

***

There is a knock on the door. Magda opens. A woman in her late thirties stands before her. A thin flow of silver streaks her black hair. 'I'm back,' says Romina. 'Can I come in?'

Magda steps aside. Her right hand trembles. Then she reaches out to the woman and they fall into each other's arms.

'I read about Jan Palach in the papers,' Romina says.

Magda is silent.

'They have flowers at the place, and his photo.'

'It has become a sort of shrine.'

'To freedom.'

'Freedom means different things to different people. He died in protest. Almost at the same spot Jiři was killed.'

'And you still live here?'

'I pay the rent. Always did.'

'I saw the light. You at the window.'

'I know.'

'Did you know it was me?'

'Not straight away.'

'But you were watching.'

'Yes.'

'Won't you offer me some wine?'

Magda blushes. 'Of course. Please take your coat off. You must be hungry. Go inside. Things have changed a little, but not much.'

Romina looks past the door from the kitchen. 'A sofa instead of mattresses on the floor,' she says as she takes off her coat and lays it across Magda's outstretched arm.

Magda laughs.

Magda fetches two crystal goblets of dark red wine balanced on a tray with a plate of black rye bread slices smeared thickly with paprika cheese. On a board is a knife and some half-cut sausage. As she places the tray on the small table beside the sofa their eyes meet. Magda's hand tremours and Romina leans forward to steady the tray, her own hand brushing Magda's fingers. An electric bond holds the two women for a long moment.

Magda clears her throat. Strokes it. Feels her pulse race beneath a telltale vein throbbing, as if awakened.

'Magda?'

Magda looks at Romina whose lips seemed to glisten like the ripe flesh of a spliced pomegranate.

'Have you lived all alone since Jiři was killed?'

Magda hands Romina a goblet of wine and clinks her glass against it. 'I've never forgotten,' she says and sips.

'The day the tanks came?'

'And the day before.'

'I've been unable to forget ...'

Magda brushes her hand over her lap as if to smooth ripples in her velvet gown.

'The look on your face when Jiři and I were making love.'

Magda reaches for her wine. The vein at her throat pulses wildly.

'You have the same look, Magda,' Romina says and places her goblet back on the tray. Her hand covers Magda's and her fingers stroke Magda's thigh. 'It feels good.'

Magda is still, wills herself into inaction as the telltale vein dances.

'Put your glass down,' Romina says.

Magda obeys and as if released, leans into the sofa. The down hairs on her arms tingle as Romina moves closer, turns and almost leans into and over her. Romina's finger strokes Magda's cheek, slips down her jawbone and traces the length of the throbbing vein. Magda closes her eyes.

'Hush,' Romina says. She strokes to that dip in Magda's throat before pursuing its gentle course over her clavicle. 'It's your wing bone, your wish bone.'

'It's been so long,' Magda whispers.

'I know,' says Romina as her hands push away the bodice of Magda's gown. 'You want this, don't you?'

Magda's eyes are wide now, almost pleading. She does not answer.

Romina gazes at Magda's full breasts straining against the black lace of her bra. 'You pamper yourself, underneath,' Romina whispers, and gently rolls the crest of Chantilly back from the nub of a nipple. 'Anticipation is half of it,' she croons. Her finger circles the puckered areola, round and around. Then she brings her finger to her lips, sucks it and returns to attend to the nipple.

Magda groans and, arching her back, pulls the lace down from her other breast.

'They are magnificent,' Romina says.

'Suck me,' Magda says. 'Please suck me. That's what you said to Jiři.'

Romina sits up and her eyes caress Magda's face in the same way her fingers explored her throat and her breast. 'Indeed, my lovely. Indeed. But first let me become a little free.'

Magda half lies on the sofa, her breasts exposed, spilling over, and watches as Romina slips out of her jumper and unbuttons her blouse.

'I don't believe in underwear anymore,' says Romina and leans over Magda, her own full breasts swaying.

'What do you believe in?'

Romina kisses Magda, her lips parting to coax Magda's now eager tongue.

'Tell me about the mangrove,' Magda whispers.

Romina's hand drifts over Magda's belly and rolls down the lace of her panties, her fingers tangling in Magda's warm brush. They twirl and tug gently at the springy hairs. 'The rain forest is damp and the rich soil stifles beneath vines and undergrowth.' Romina's voice is hypnotic as is the motion of her fingers, tugging, kneading, gently exploring Magda's lush mound. 'The fingers of mangrove, long roots, undulating, are all that can free the way to the ocean.'

Suddenly, Romina grasps the knife from the tray and rips through the gusset of Magda's panties. Magda catches her breath. Her heart races.

'But sometimes there are vines that need to be cut away.' She places the knife back on the tray and continues her ministrations. 'The silt of the mangrove is unctuous,' she says as she plunges two fingers into Magda's cunt.

Magda groans, more loudly now, her tongue slowly licking her lips.

Romina straddles Magda's thighs and with her free hand tucks her skirt in her waistband and then combs her long fingers through her own brush. 'See how the mangrove is lush,' she says as she parts her rich lips.

Magda's hand reaches out, her fingers meet Romina's and follow to explore the thick wetness.

'What was it you said to Jiři?' Magda asks hoarsely.

'Suck harder.'

Magda leans over Romina's hand now pushing and thrusting into her core. She parts Romina's full lips and the pulsing ripe fruit fills her mouth as she darts her tongue and sucks, luxuriating in the primal perfume.

Romina writhes, screams then hums. 'The ocean fills and wave upon wave crashes onto the mangrove,'

Magda moans and opens her gown for Romina to cleave against her breast.

The next day there are demonstrations at Wenceslas Square.

'It is for freedom,' Magda says.

'I don't want to go,' says Romina.

The day after, Romina is still adamant.

'We must go. For Jiři,' Magda says.

'It's been twenty years. Stay here with me and the freedom of the mangrove.'

The third day Romina accedes.

'It will be over soon,'.

The women walk arm in arm over the Charles Bridge. They stop at the brass plaque. 'I don't need to wish anymore,' Magda says.

'Just one rub,' says Romina as she kisses her friend on the cheek and takes off her glove.

Magda smiles and shakes her head. 'Is that what you believe in?'

As they near Wenceslas Square there are throngs of demonstrators calling out for the release of dissidents. The police advances. People run. Arms flail. Truncheons smash down. A rifle butt swipes Magda's head. She falls. Blood gashes from her forehead, the vein at her throat suddenly pulsates.

Romina sinks to the ground and cradles her lover. Magda stares, her voice just a whisper. 'True freedom?'

Romina's eyes glisten with breaking tears. 'Somewhere between the rainforest and the ocean,' she answers. Magda shudders and is then still.

***

Romina left Prague, unaware that the 'velvet revolution' had already begun. She returned ten years later on a tourist pilgrimage of sorts. Her hotel TV brought weather reports with images of naked men and women moderators. The whispers that under repression had screamed their urgent need now were mere murmurs of acceptance.

Picnic at Niagara

They say that the weather can change in Niagara, so it was important to come well prepared.

A bottle of Nuits-St-Georges, a jar of plump Spanish mussels, and a small box of hand-made dark truffle chocolates are the things that I'll bring. And two glasses, a corkscrew and large serviettes. The serviettes are paper, but of good quality in the lush yellow and blue of my home in Provence. I'll be wearing new clothes: a crossover top that might show a glimpse of black lace edging the Bordeaux of my bra. The top is not tight, but the fabric clings just enough for my nipples to show their change of humour. It should be warm and sunny so I'll wear a mid-knee-length skirt in a soft floral that I can push up gently should I feel the need to slightly spread my legs. But he won't be able to see my new clothes, for I'll still have my coat on; it is early and we'll not yet have found the place for our picnic. I do hope we find an appropriate place, perhaps an abandoned path to the rapids. I must remember to take some mules, ones I can slip in and out of with ease.

Rich liver *paté*, a ripe creamy Brie, a fresh French baguette are the things that he'll bring. His grey herringbone jacket is pure wool against the breeze. I'm sure he has also thought of the weather. But he'll wear an open-neck shirt which will be slightly darker in tone than the blue of his eyes. We are between seasons and I can imagine the feel of his mustard cord pants. He has forgotten to go to the hairdresser this month and I like the way his thick grey hair touches his shirt collar at the back.

I'll follow him, a little blindly, yet trusting. I know he will find the perfect spot: a rough wooden table with two benches under the trees down by the lake away from the crowds in a place where we can feel the mist rising. I imagine the noise of the waterfall rushing, tumbling down, but we are too far for it to be a distraction. What I do hear is my own thrill and excitement. I wonder if he can hear it as well. It is as though I am looking in from the outside, a voyeur on a secret time of my life.

We are the picture of old-world decorum. I spread out two of the lush serviettes. He has a penknife, but we have forgotten plates. We laugh at this part of our impracticality. I place the bottle of deep red wine on the table. He takes it and considers the label. 'The proof of the wine is in the drinking,' is what he says.

I smile and place the glasses on the rough wooden table. He unpacks the *paté*, the cheese and the bread. I hand him the corkscrew.

It is getting warmer and I take off my coat. He opens the bottle, but his eyes are upon me. I feel his approval and it makes me start to blush and, as if he has noticed, he turns his eyes once more to the task of the bottle. What he cannot see is the sensual contrast: the warmth of my blush and the feel of a spring breeze beneath my skirt. I'm wearing lace panties, black over Bordeaux, sheer, the mid-seam unsewn, a personal compromise between a thong and nothing at all.

The cork pops and from his gaze I can see that my nipples betray me and hint at the thrill coming beneath. There is a swirling, a turmoil, as the Falls tumble over. Again. And again.

We sit face to face, the table between us. He raises the screwed cork to his nostrils and breathes in the trapped bouquet. He closes his eyes for a moment before filling our glasses and then, raising his in a toast, he says, 'Here's to what's happening.'

I cannot speak. I just nod and I sip. He breaks the bread and cuts some *paté*, spreads it on the dough of the baguette and hands it to me. I take the morsel and our fingers meet. I cannot resist drawing his fingers to my lips. My tongue touches the bread and *paté* as my lips enclose the morsel and swallow, I draw him into my mouth just far enough to nibble, imperceptibly suckle. I cannot be calm and so break the spell. 'Shall we play a game?' I ask.

His index finger wanders to my lips and traces the fragile moist skin. His finger lingers and I close my eyes. Then he withdraws his hand and spreads some Brie. 'I'm game,' he says. We both know the rules. We do not want complications. Yet we are like children before an adventure. I lean forward for the jar of mussels and the movement catches his eye. His gaze lingers on my taut nipples. I open the jar. With two fingers I catch a slippery mussel. 'They are Spanish.'

He nods. 'This one looks familiar,' he says as he considers the folds of the two luscious lips. 'There's a pearl there,' he adds and, as if as an afterthought: 'I wonder if you are as I imagine.'

I suddenly feel a throb deep and low in that part of me he cannot see, below the table. A moistness. I part my legs in the hope that a zephyr might cool what is happening. I sip and feel wine on my lips. 'Do you have fantasies?' I hear myself say. He nods. I am silent. Then he takes the mussel from my fingers and lets it slide into his mouth. I watch him, imagine a scene, and he says: 'Please share yours with me.'

A couple approaches and with an envious glance at the food on our table move past us down to the lake. I hear the Falls thunder, hold my breath, breathe out slowly.

'So tell me,' he says.

We wait until we are alone. The couple has gone, no doubt to look more closely at the thundering Falls and watch the power of the river vibrating. I have my own turmoil and wonder what he would do if I came around to his side of the table.

My fantasy is to be here with you. The food we have brought has just served as a prelude. I straddle the bench; you turn to face me. My skirt rides up, but still covers my thighs. I keep still and wait for you to move. You smile and stroke my cheek with your finger, then my neck. My nipples strain against my bra and blouse. You gently pull one side of the crossover top away; my bra is sheer and you push the black lace a little so that just the nipple peeks over it. I remain still but my pulse rushes, is racing. I feel flushed.

Suddenly the light changes as clouds gather above us. A solitary drop falls. You lick your finger and rub the wet over my exposed nipple. The cool air makes it hard. I want you, but I do not move. You take your time, paying scant heed to the tightening clouds. You obviously enjoy watching me unable to stir. You take off your jacket and spread it over the remains of the spoils on our table. Then you straddle the bench and you face me.

A bulge starts to strain your pants. I pretend I don't see it, but I do. It makes me hot, but I keep still. You move closer to me and your hand pushes back my skirt. You stare and I watch the bulge in your pants. You have seen the slit in the lace of my panties. Your finger strokes my inside thigh and then hovers over the lacy slit. I am trying not to gasp. Gently your finger enters the lacy opening and urges further between the Chantilly of my brush. I am wet. Thickly wet. You like this. You draw out your finger and hold it, slightly slanted, beneath your nostrils. You breathe in and half close your eyes. Imperceptibly you smile and slowly suck on your finger. I close my eyes. You have teased me and told me what it could be like, but it is much more than I ever could have imagined. You are driving me wild.

'I love the taste of you,' you say. 'I want to suck that pearl of yours and lick your darling mussel folds. Lie back,' you tell me, and I do. You spread my legs and gaze at my open swollen pussy, then your head comes down and in long strong licks you burrow your face into me. Sucking, nibbling my clit, slurping as if unable to get enough of my juices. I can't believe you're doing this to me.

You want to be there when I come. You want to taste it. And I do come. The clouds are breaking over Niagara and I come in waves, in clutches. Rain falls in plump warm drops as you lap all the while, lapping and stroking until the wild flow of the rapids suffuses to a satisfied calm… Then you pull me up and grin. I wipe your mouth with my fingers and kiss your lips, tasting me all over them. We caress gently, but even the lake has undercurrents of longing. The sun pierces the clouds as we kiss and drink from each other's mouths once more, tonguing, nibbling, and sucking. I look down and reach out to unzip you. 'We mustn't be cruel,' I say.

You help with your belt and I free your bulging cock. You stand and face me now. I want my fill. I take this dear part of you—there is no foreskin as I had imagined—and stroke and lick the shaft as your hands hold my head and guide me. I lick the knob—a droplet—tasting of sea, inland and salty. I want more and flick my tongue about that little slit and gently suck for more. You are tensing. I hear your breathing. I cannot stop sucking, drawing your delicious cock deep into my mouth, slurping, wanting to draw from deep within you. I cannot stop. You are moaning now. I take your balls and fondle and squeeze them. You cannot hold back now, although you are trying. You are rushing to the edge. I want you to come. I am prepared. I don't want to waste a precious drop. And there it is. The gush of your force is more than I dreamed. I swallow rhythmically as your essence flows and then fills me. I look up to you, my lips lingering on the tip of your knob and give a final tender lick.

You wipe my mouth with your fingers and draw me to you. We hold each other, kissing languidly and long, tasting the last of a delicious lunch. You begin to straighten my top and give my nipple one last quick suckle. I zip your pants. We are both soaking and thank the weather. You take your jacket and we clear up. So well behaved, we know what we must do. You hand me the penknife and the corkscrew and I wipe them clean with the damp serviettes. Next time, we both know, there will be much more than just an appetizer in the park.

I sit in the lobby of my New York hotel. Water gushes down a decorative wall. It is meant to be soothing, but it pounds like the Falls where we were to have met. A page cries: 'Mrs Benoit. A call for you.'

I have been waiting and was so well prepared. An appetizer usually leads to a main course. But the wild card of a flight cancellation has wiped out our only window of time. Now all that remains is this last call across one of so many bodies of water.

'I'm sorry,' I say.

'I'm sorry too.'

'It was a wonderful lunch, though.'

'You will write and tell me about it?'

'Yes,' I whisper. 'I will write and the words will make it true. Anyway, I still have the dark chocolate truffles.'

'Then slip one in your mouth for me, darling.'

'Yes, I shall do that. Yes, yes and yes.'

Just Lunch

She didn't trust words, at least not those that came out of people's mouths. She trusted the ones on the page. She could keep those, turn them over, dissect them and look for their true meanings. An island lives in the sea, she thought, as she dipped into the wide waters of the web and surfed into a forum for matters literary. It was there that the young woman from Crescent Street, Montreal met a man who spoke her language; it didn't matter that he was older and that he came from Mississauga—young men had burned her and Mississauga was far enough for comfort.

They discussed stories, his and hers, and books by others, and one afternoon, for that seemed to be the best time for them both, they slipped out of the group and into email. 'How about lunch,' he wrote. She didn't answer straight away. Lunch. A meal at noontime. Daylight. Can't speak while you're eating, it would be rude. Somewhere provincial where nothing could happen. What could happen? It was just lunch.

Now, five months later, she stood at the market and surveyed the stalls. Asparagus tips? Tomatoes? Rocket? Lunch had been easy the first time.

The first time was in Windsor. He'd fetched her at the station and they went to a restaurant where the road was dug up. She'd imagined him bearded, but he was clean shaven. Can I taste your bumble berry pie, she asked as her spoon hovered in the air. Indeed, he replied. Indeed you can. They didn't speak much, their eyes did the talking. She said she'd stay overnight. He said he couldn't, had to get back to Mississauga. It was named by the French, she said. I know, he replied and gave her a hardback, Alice Munro's *The Love of a Good Woman*. In her B&B room she devoured the stories, looking for signs.

What would she need? Chives and herbes de provence. Some good wine, red and white. Chablis? Bordeaux?

The second time was in Stratford. He was a great fan of Timothy Findley. They saw his *Elizabeth Rex* and lunched late at Pazzo's. 'Did you know Tiff and his partner ate here? They lived upstairs.' She hadn't known. He ordered ice wine. 'The grapes are the last before the frost. That's why it's so sweet,' he said. She felt as if they were on some invisible plank, needing each other just to walk it.

Two chocolate truffles, individually wrapped, and a flask of Armagnac.

The third time was in Lincoln. They sat in a park by the Falls and picnicked on the *paté* and baguette she'd brought from the Crescent Street market. They hardly spoke. She gave him a story she'd downloaded. 'Love's

Lesson' by Edna O'Brien. A bit erotic, a bit on the side. A bit sad. As he read he stroked the inside of her wrist.

At the baker's she bought a fresh baguette; at the butcher's a small fillet of beef; at the fishmonger's two large sea urchins. She still had some sour cream.

The fourth time was in Thamesford. He'd just had his first scan. Over sashimi she read him a story she'd written. 'You're dead below the neck', he said. She couldn't speak, not then, not later when he slipped a slim book into her hands: Epictetus' *The Art of Living*; and when he said *au revoir*, she said nothing.

She smoothed out the ivory Richelieu linen and set the table with her fine bone china, two crystal glasses, two serviettes.

The last time was London. 'Don't come,' he messaged. 'My mouth's full of sores.' She didn't answer. 'But my mind is famished; let me know what you're eating.' She hesitated and then typed back: Lunch is on me.

She lit a scented white candle and placed it into a silver holder.

She would tell him about the lunch she'd prepared, the meal that they'd had. How she'd scooped the soft flesh of the sea urchins and fed him gently. How he'd sipped the Chablis and sucked on grape tomatoes and asparagus tips. How the beef had been rare and had melted like butter. (He'd passed on the Bordeaux and she'd let it be.) How she'd unwrapped the truffles and poured him a tear of Armagnac. How they'd listened for rain, but it had stayed fine. She would tell him how much he'd enjoyed it, how he'd noticed the scent of frangipani, and how he'd stayed on for dinner.

It was only much later alone in her bed, when her fingers had ceased thrusting, that she gave in and finally let herself cry.

Matilda's Waltz

Matilda Flaherty stood on the veranda of the low-roofed house and scanned the dry grassland. A black speck flickered in the band of heat quivering over the yellow horizon. It was moving too swiftly to be a man on foot. That bloody McFarland, she said aloud as she rolled down the sleeves of her white lawn blouse. The horseman cantered towards the house and came to a halt in a maelstrom of dust.

'Morning, Mrs Flaherty,' the man said as he tipped his hat. 'Any news from Jack?'

Matilda's face was hot. Jack had been gone three months now and she'd been managing as best she could. And she would continue for as long as it took. 'You know he wasn't counting on less than four or five months, Mr McFarland.'

'Three's already a stretch,' the man said as he dismounted. 'Call me Ron, won't you?' he said as he

AstridL

stroked his thoroughbred's drenched flanks. 'It's been a long enough stretch without rain.' A bead of sweat trickled down Matilda's neck. 'You feeling the heat, Mrs. Flaherty?'

Matilda cursed under her breath.

'What was that?' he said in a low voice as his eyes followed the droplet's glistening course. 'Would you not have something to quench a man's thirst, Mrs Flaherty?'

Matilda turned on her heel. 'Cold tea,' she threw back at him. 'Can you wait on the veranda?'

In the kitchen, Matilda mopped her neck and breast. If she buttoned her blouse, he would be sure his gaze had had an effect. If she didn't, it would be inviting his greedy stare to linger. She breathed deeply a couple of times then grabbed a pitcher of tea from the stone floor. To hell with McFarland, she thought. Let him get an eyeful. That would be all the bastard would be getting, she thought as she scooped up a mug from the sink and went out to the veranda. She stopped in the doorway. McFarland was sitting in the old armchair she'd just finished upholstering with deep green velvet. It was to be a surprise for Jack. Now McFarland was in it. She wanted to tell him to get out, wanted to scream at him, but she had to stay calm. She'd give him his drink and then he'd be off, she thought as she placed the pitcher on the floor by the armchair and handed McFarland the mug.

'Not joining me, Mrs Flaherty?' McFarland said as he leant over, grasped the pitcher, and poured the liquid into his mug.

Matilda stood with a hand propped against the wall. 'I'll be fine,' she said. 'What brings you out this way in the heat?'

'Just some neighbourly concern, Mrs Flaherty. A body worries what with a young woman alone in the bush.'

'That's good of you,' Matilda said trying to keep the sarcasm out of her voice, 'but I can take good care of myself.'

McFarland nodded and licked his lip before taking another gulp of the tea. 'Well, if there's anything you'll be needing?' His eyes ran over her shoulders, lingered on her bodice and then flashed over her unbuttoned cuffs.

Matilda smoothed the cuff over one wrist and shook her head. 'I have chores to attend to, Mr McFarland.'

'Seems you've been attending to some extras,' he said, stroking the side of the armchair with his free hand. 'Nice work,' he said. 'Comfortable, too.' Then he rose and handed her the mug, his rough fingers grazing her hand. 'If there's anything you'll be needing?' he said slowly, his eyes now fixed on a tiny throbbing vein at her throat.

Matilda gripped the mug and bent to pick up the pitcher. She wanted to throw it at him, but she kept her voice steady. 'Thank you, Mr McFarland,' she said as she straightened up. 'I'll be fine.'

McFarland shrugged, hesitated a moment and then went to his horse. He stroked a hand over the black mare's rump and then mounted it. Sitting straight in the saddle, he turned away from the house and then his head pivoted around. 'Lost half the stock already, Mrs Flaherty. Like all the others. Don't suppose Jack will have found much work with this drought.'

'Good bye, Mr McFarland,' Matilda said.

'Thanks for the drink,' McFarland said and as his horse broke into a trot he added, 'Let me know when you're ready, Matilda.' Then he rode off up the hill spewing dust clouds behind him.

Matilda stood on the veranda gripping the pitcher with both hands. Angry tears wet her cheeks. She wiped them away with the back of one hand and stormed into the kitchen.

***

Hours later, the night was still hot. Matilda lay on the bed and stared at Jack's straw hat above the door. He'd taken the leather one, the stockman's hat. The straw one he'd said was for the gentleman farmer, for when he'd be back, lounging in a comfortable armchair on the veranda. She'd promised to fan him with the straw hat. It was their joke, and their dream, and now it hung on a hook on the wall.

The drought had killed off a good part of the flock and Matilda knew McFarland was just waiting for the rest to go so that he could stake his claim on the Flaherty property. McFarland could bloody well go to hell. 'Oh, Jack,' Matilda cried. 'Please come back soon.' Tears welled in her eyes. 'It is so hot. Will you fan me?'

She slipped off her nightdress. Moonlight dappled the room through the shadows of the leaves of the lone gum tree outside the window. The night was warm and still smelled of dust. She reached for the hat, lay down and fanned.

Three months is so long, she thought. She fanned herself rhythmically, cooling the air above her in waves, back and forth, back and forth. Then the hat grazed a nipple and Matilda lay electrified. Too long, Jack. She moved the hat's brim from left to right over her breasts. 'Jack,' she cried out. 'Look what your gentleman hat is doing,' she whispered, 'it's driving them wild.' No, I shan't crush it. I'm turning it over. My fist is now in its crown. So delightful the prickle of its straw. Yes, down. It's tangling. No, I won't crush it. Do you mind if it has become just a little damp? The smell is so rich. A delicious sop, my darling. Imagine, pearl juice on fresh straw.

Matilda slept deeply, the hat by her side. She dreamt of gentle rains and rolling green land. Orange roses were in full bloom and their cinnamon scent filled the air. She fanned Jack on the veranda and then they withdrew to the bedroom, to make love, yes, sweet gentle love, and outside all the while lambs were gently bleating.

Matilda awoke to the loud bleat of sheep. She leapt into her long cotton robe and dashed outside. The last of the flock were running blind up the hill a scrawny cattle dog at their hooves. At the top of the hill stood a lone rider.

Matilda ripped at her hair and screamed out Jack's name to the burnt grass. She had promised to hang on. What was left now? The land? Only the land? Jack would come. Jack. Where are you?

***

Ron McFarland stood at the bar in the Kynuna Hotel, one foot propped on the side of the copper spittoon. His slouch hat covered one eyebrow. 'Got a good price,' he said.

'Blood lucky,' said the publican. 'They say the drought'll be easing soon.'

The policeman sucked on his beer. 'Good thing we nabbed the swaggie, though.'

'Yes,' said McFarland. 'He'd stolen a jumbuck. They may look like clouds, but they're our bread and butter. Didn't believe a word, eh officer? Said he was just down the billabong boiling a billy. Was on his way home.'

'A swaggie ain't got a home,' said the publican. 'Just his swag. Reckon they hump 'em.'

'For lack of anything better,' said McFarland. 'Which reminds me, any news about Jack Flaherty?'

The publican shook his head. 'What's he got to come back to?'

'Indeed,' McFarland said.

'All his stock gone, and his missus gone crazed.'

'That land'll just go to waste,' said McFarland.

'Nothing you can do about that,' said the policeman. 'Matilda Flaherty is staying put. Says Jack will be back.'

'She's mad,' said the publican. 'Hear she goes for walks in the night. Down to the billabong.'

'Does she now,' McFarland said. 'Maybe it's time for another neighbourly visit.'

'You having designs, Ron?' the policeman said with a grin.

'Maybe. Maybe not. She's a good-looking woman with a nice piece of … land. I could be of help.'

The men sniggered. 'Now what sort of help would you have in mind then?' the policeman said.

'Just a helping hand,' McFarland said with a long wink. 'Wouldn't want her to lose it completely.'

'I'd watch it Ron,' the publican said 'She's got a husband soon to be on his way home. Jack Flaherty can get red hot.'

'What do you take me for?' McFarland said. 'I've got time on my side.' He took his foot from the spittoon, leant over and spat.

***

The heat eased off and every day more and more clouds were beginning to form. What at first had resembled white fluffy sheep now even looked like a promise of rain. Matilda trudged towards the house pulling a small trolley with a sack of flour and sugar, and a box of tea. She'd done the two miles to and from town on foot. She'd had to stock up, just in case Jack needed longer. She hoisted the sacks onto the kitchen table and put the box of loose tea in the pantry.

'Poor bugger,' she thought. Mrs Keen at the store had told her the news about the swaggie they'd shot at. McFarland and his police goons in action again, Matilda had thought. 'Seems he got away,'

Matilda couldn't help thinking about the swaggie. Maybe he's still hiding out in the bush. Maybe he's wounded, she thought. Jack would help a bloke like that. Anyway, with the sheep gone, all she could do was wait; but the waiting was driving her crazy. Matilda rolled a swag with a blanket and packed some tea in an old billy can. As an afterthought, she took the straw hat and put it on. A good fan for tonight, she thought. I'll camp out. Change of scenery. Maybe I'll find him.

She walked up the hill and turned to look back at the house with its low roofed veranda. It was all they had now, that and the land. Over the hill the sparse bushland thickened downwards. Tall eucalyptus stood like sentries, dried bracken between them. A tinderbox, Matilda thought. But rain would come soon. She pushed her way through the scrub that now welcomed large ferns. She was coming closer to water. She could smell it. And then past a clearing she saw the bank of the billabong where the water was still. She unrolled her blanket and set about gathering bracken and wood scraps for a fire. When she had enough to keep burning a fire for an hour or so, she arranged it in a heaped pile and then took the billy can to fetch water. In the same way that daylight cracked without dawn, so too fell the night and soon the moon played through the whispering gums. The bush was alive with sounds of scuttling in the undergrowth. Down by the water the earth smelled yeasty damp. She squatted and dipped the can into the water and then she froze. Someone was there. She heard a keening, a soft wailing. It was if someone were singing.

'You'll never take me alive,' the deep voice sang.

She knew that voice.

'Come waltz, my Matilda, come with me.'

Jack. It was Jack. She dropped the billy. 'Jack,' she called.

There were footsteps behind her. A shadow. She spun round, into the arms of Ron McFarland. 'Let me go,' she screamed.

'Mrs Flaherty, Matilda, calm down now,' McFarland said. 'It's a danger to be out in the bush at night all alone.'

Matilda knelt to pick up the billy and stood stiffly. 'I am not alone, Mr McFarland. Jack is here.'

McFarland stretched out an arm, knocked off her hat and clasped her jaw with one hand, grabbing at her breast with the other. 'Jack is dead, Matilda,' he said through his teeth.

Matilda stood shock still, her breasts heaving.

'Nice,' growled McFarland as his large hand tried to cover them and his open mouth came down on hers. Matilda bit into his tongue and squirmed out of his grasp. She swung the billy still in her hand and caught him on the side of the head.

'You,' he spat and lunged after her, dragging at her as she reached for the blanket which she bunched under her belly. His body crushed hers over the blanket and she fell face down.

'They say the swaggies do it with the sheep. You'd know all about that, now, wouldn't you Matilda?' McFarland's hand was under her skirt, plying her buttocks.

Matilda bucked and tried to lunge out of his hold but his hands were now firmly on her hips. He pinned her down and Matilda felt she would explode for lack of air and the anger and fear and the tears. 'Jack,' she prayed. Pretend it's Jack, she thought. Mind over matter. Pretend it's Jack losing control. Help him. Her fingers grabbed between her legs and she rubbed and rubbed.

McFarland growled, she could hear his urgent breathing over her back. Faster. Get there before him. He was freeing himself. She had to be there first. Her fingers wet, she stretched her hand further back and slipped one, then, two fingers into that sweet dark crack that Jack had but once explored. She was winning. Out now. Let him plunge now. Jack.

'A right little jumback,' McFarland said hoarsely. 'You done this before, me lovely,' he wheedled and then plunged in, in, out, in, in. 'Not your first time, eh. That's for sure.'

But Matilda didn't hear him. She was gone, she was with her Jack. He'd gone over the edge and she with him. He was deep now, so deep she could hear him. 'It's ok, love,' he was saying. 'It's ok.'

When Matilda came to, McFarland had gone. He'd said something, the last that she'd heard. What was it? What was it? Come? Come round?

'So you came round after all, Matilda Flaherty. I'll be back for more then, my little jumbuck. Would've got you one way or the other.' Matilda's heart thumped wildly in her throat. That's what he'd said. No fear, she thought. She grabbed at the blanket and the crushed straw hat. She couldn't go back to the house now. She dragged herself off a way behind a clump of bracken and sat, ears pricked, listening to the scurrying sounds of the bush night. Then she rolled the blanket about her and sobbed silently. Jack. Jack.

'Come a waltzing with me,' a gentle voice sang through the night, and Matilda was calmed and she slept.

Jack's arms were around her. He stroked her and kissed her. His gentle hands soothed her. She fanned him. Trailed kisses down his neck and his chest. She licked his navel so salty and sweet. That yeasty fragrance. She couldn't stop. She sucked and she sucked and the pearl juice dribbled onto the soft straw. And then Jack turned her over, caressed her once more, and she knew that he was home, home at last.

***

The next morning Ron McFarland rode out to the Flaherty house. The door and the windows were closed. He grinned. Still out in the bush, he thought. A little daytime go at it. Ha. He galloped over the hill and down the other side towards the billabong. The billy can lay by the dead embers of what had been a campfire. Matilda's skirt and blouse, her socks and boots, white bloomers, too, lay in a heap. McFarland smiled. 'Now where's that jolly jumbuck?' he sang. He went down to the water. It was still. Tiny insects buzzed out of reach as he dipped his hand in the water and squinted. If she's swimming, I'd see her. Maybe she's gone down the other end. But so far with no clothes? She must be crazy. McFarland spat. Jack Flaherty was dead. He'd said it. She must have gone raving into the bush. They said she'd gone mad. He gazed over the clearing and back to the billabong. If he wanted the land he'd need a witness. A police report.

He'd been doing his neighbourly duty, checking to see if Matilda Flaherty hadn't been needing anything, he later told the policeman. We have to find her, she might be in danger. 'You're a good bloke, Ron McFarland', the policeman had said.

***

They found Matilda Flaherty face down at the far end of the billabong. She was naked except for a blanket tangled around one thigh. When they turned her over, she had a smile on her face. In the water a few yards away, they found a crushed straw hat and a leather stockman's one floating beside it. To this day, they say there are ghosts in the billabong. They say that they sing. The same song. The same song.

Hannah's Revenge

Hannah cupped her left breast and stared at the bathroom mirror. The breast showed no sign of the odd heartbeat that had been sending painful jabs through her body, and had been making her catch her breath more and more lately. The breast was full and plump; a brown nipple peeped out between index and middle finger. Her midriff was trim for her thirty-nine years, her hips generous yet fairly firm. The brush on her pubis was still russet and lush – she'd never succumbed to Brazilian. But now was the time to shave it all off. She ran a bath and went to the window looking over the leafy promenade that meandered alongside the banks of the canal.

Hans would soon come jogging along. She'd been watching him for a week now. He'd come down to the water at ten, stretch a little to warm up and then take off through the promenade. It had kept him trim and tanned. He hadn't really changed that much over the years. She'd been sitting on the bench in the clearing when he first jogged by. He hadn't recognised her. He'd seen a woman he'd wanted to see and had followed his old tactics. Ignore them first, ignore them again, sooner or later they'll be eating out of your hand, he'd said it ten years ago. He'd said it to Wolfgang. The sorcerer and his apprentice.

Hans had been a sorcerer all right. Viennese charm. Smooth. He'd had a way and he'd tried it with Hannah, but Hannah didn't do dirty old men then, although it was close. Close enough for Hans to see her snatch as she uncrossed her legs. Hannah loved going naked down under on hot summer days and thrilled to the feel of a breeze on her cunt, a place she rarely let older men go. Hans wasn't that old back then, end forties. But he was too old for her twenty-nine.

'Real russet,' Hans said, and Hannah pulled her knees together.

'No,' she said.

'Not me, my love,' he wheedled back. 'I'm attending to the education of my nephew. How about showing him. No touch.'

'You're sick,' she retorted.

'He's nineteen,' Hans said. 'Think about it.'

Hannah was silent a moment.

'Well?'

'A virgin?' she asked.

Hans nodded.

Hannah met Wolfgang in the park further down from the promenade. He was gangly and fresh faced with excitement. Hannah took his hand and led him to a bench.

'Let's sit and chat,' she said, smoothing her flounced skirt over her thighs.

Wolfgang watched her hands as she smoothed the flounces and then crossed her legs. There was no breeze, but Hannah could feel a tensing in her belly.

'Do you like swings?' she said.

Wolfgang looked puzzled.

'There's one over there. Will you push me?' Wolfgang nodded and Hannah took his hand and led him to the playground. 'I'm a little scared,' she said. 'I always was as a child. But if you come round the other side after you've given me a push …'

'I can catch you in case you fall?'

'Yes'

Wolfgang pushed Hannah and up she swung. As she came down, he was on the other side ready to catch her as promised. Her skirt billowed up to expose her lush russet bush. Wolfgang stood staring, his arms open wide and Hannah jumped from the swing straight into them. He held her a moment, or she held him, just long enough to feel he was hard. He blushed.

'Are you all right?' he asked.

'Are you?' she said with a smile.

'Why are you smiling?' Wolfgang said.

'You make me happy,' she answered. You're making me wet, darling boy, she thought. 'Do you want to come over to my place for ...'

'A drink?'

'Yes,' she said.

They made love in her studio flat. Hannah'd taken the lead and they'd laughed when things didn't go smoothly. Over the weeks, and over the months, Wolfgang became more assured. It no longer mattered to Hannah that Hans was his uncle. Hans seemed to have gone up in smoke. Puff. Wolfgang moved in.

When Wolfgang didn't come home one night, Hannah didn't think too much of it. We're free, she thought. To do as we please. I love him; he loves me.

'I love you,' said Wolfgang. His eyes were wet. 'I've been sitting on the doorstep for hours. Forgive me.' Forgive my sins. A fist worked its way up inside Hannah's stomach. Confession's the easy way out. Just say it and move on.

'Don't touch me,' she said.

Hannah didn't let Wolfgang touch her for weeks. Stories ran wildly through her head. She saw Hans with the Brazilian. Long hair, longer legs, taut, tight. Meet my nephew, he said. Drink up, Wolfy, have some fun. You've never seen a Brazilian one. Hannah'll never know, and anyway, it's part of your education. She'll thank you for it. The Brazilian took Wolfgang by the hand, led him into a small room, caressed, kissed him. Wolfy couldn't resist.

What young man could? The Brazilian's skin was smooth all the way down. Wolfy must have wondered if it was smooth down there, if it was shaved. Wolfy was hard.

The Brazilian was, too.

Red heat rushed to Wolfy's temples. He bolted. Threw up. Lunged for Hans lounging outside. 'I hate you,' he yelled.

Hans smirked. 'Part of your education, my boy.'

Time went by and days were fine. Hannah and Wolfgang never mentioned the Brazilian. Wolfgang saw Hans from time to time, but Hannah refused to see Wolfgang's uncle. Nights in bed she'd hold Wolfgang closely and rock him. Rocking made it better for him and Hannah felt that she still had time: time to wean him away from the shock of having hardened to the ministrations of a smooth shaven man, time to erase the thought of having betrayed her. It hadn't been his fault, Hannah reflected. The fault had been Hans'.

'Hans has a new motorbike,' Wolfgang said one day.

Hannah said nothing.

'I'm going to see it. Want to come?'

Hannah shook her head.

'Do you mind?'

Hannah shook her head once again.

When Hans rang to say that Wolfgang had taken a spin on the bike, that a truck had smashed him flat, that his nephew was dead, Hannah buckled over and a deep low grunt came up from her core. She retched all night. For days she just lay there. Her Wolfgang, her lover, her child. The pain was unbearable. Hannah refused calls and visits from Hans. She packed her bags and went to the station and took the first train that came. She couldn't care less if it was to Siberia.

Now ten years later, Hannah was back and stood before her mirror. The pain was almost unbearable. Moderation, they'd said. No extremes. Extremes would take a toll on her heart, they said. She had months yet, if she would exercise moderation. In her bed, she'd see how far she could go. The pain in her neck shot through as she orgasmed. She didn't have that much time now and she had to work it all out.

'Do I know you?' Hans said as he jogged by Hannah sitting on the bench.

Hannah did not look up from her book entitled 'The Joy of Sex'.

Hans jogged on the spot. 'Excuse me,' he said.

Hannah looked up.

'Do you?'

Hannah looked at him blankly and then to the cover of the book. 'Oh,' she said.

'Yes, of course.'

Hans still was jogging on the spot. 'Do you jog, I mean,' he said.

'I'm afraid my health doesn't allow it,' she said softly.

'May I sit down?'

Hannah nodded.

She could feel his eyes on her cleavage, running down her neck, her thighs to her ankles.

'Interesting book,' Hans said.

Hannah nodded. Was it possible that he still didn't recognise her?

'Gentle does it?'

'Indeed.'

'Care for a glass of Prosecco?'

'Why not?'

'You do look familiar,' Hans said.

'At our age everyone does,' Hannah said.

'So you're from Vienna?'

'No. Budapest.'

'You're German's very good.'

'My mother was German, I studied,' she said.

'Guess you're right about everyone looking familiar,' he said.

'You've been with a lot of women?'

'I do my best,' Hans said and laughed as he reached an arm over her shoulder.

Hannah smiled and left it alone.

'What about that Prosecco?' she said.

In Hans' room she slowly unbuttoned her dress and let it slip to the floor. Hans lay on his bed with his arms propped behind his head. He just stared and his member saluted.

'I've a weakness for Brazilian,' he said. 'But I love it all the way.'

'I'm Hungarian,' Hannah said and stroked her smooth pubis, parting her lips to let the tip of her clit peep out between her fingers.'

'Are you naturally red?' Hans groaned. 'When it grows out, I mean?'

Hannah nodded and stroked her clit. It was swelling nicely now and her fingers were wet.

Hans eased back his foreskin. 'I knew a redhead once,' he said absently. 'But you're nothing like her. She went crazy. Probably dead.'

'That's a great comparison,' Hannah said as she straddled him and began licking his nipples.

'Wind me up, honey, and I'll make it worth your while hanging out with an old man.'

'A dirty old man,' Hannah said and gave a low grating laugh.

Hans turned her over and spread her legs. His nose nuzzled her smooth lips and bored into her cunt. He came up for breath, stared into her heart and licked his lips before plunging again.

Hannah felt a tightening in her core. Let go, she thought, as he swirled his tongue, sucking and slathering.

She could smell herself on his lips as he came up for air. Let the throbbing get stronger. Her pulse jolted in syncopation, and as he pulled at her nipples her mouth opened wide.

'She was nothing like you,' he groaned as he thrust his cock into her mouth. Hannah was prepared. She sucked for her life, or rather her death. At the last minute Hans pulled out and entered her.

'Pump away,' Hannah groaned. She could feel herself on the edge. The pain in her neck was at a threshold she'd never before reached.

More. More. And then she'd be over. Not yet. She could feel it coming. She saw the long tunnel.

Wolfy was standing, his arms open wide. 'Let' swing,' he was calling. 'I'm coming,' she screamed and collapsed like a rag doll.

Hans stroked her face. 'She was never like you,' he whispered.

Through half-closed eyes, Hannah saw stars. A sweet heavy scent wrapped itself around her like the doona she'd shared with Wolfgang.

Her eyes ripped open.

'This is for the bike, and the Brazilian,' she whispered hoarsely.

Recognition flickered in Hans' face, his mouth twisted. Hannah's lips froze in a smile as she saw the fear in his eyes. Then she slumped back.

I'm coming, dear Love, Wolfgang, my darling.

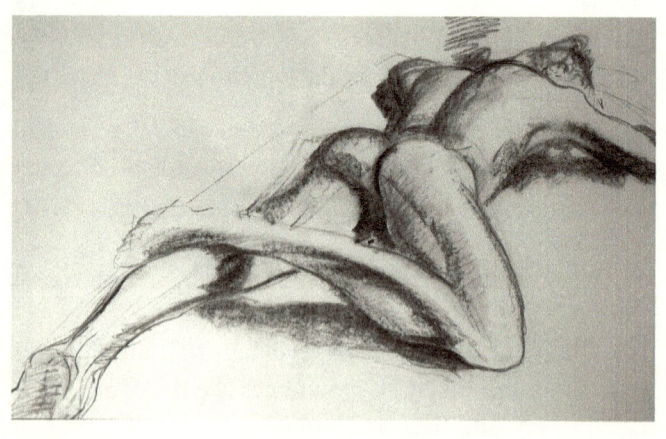

The Wages of Bliss

Light fell in dapples through the leaves of the willows by my secret pool in the glade by the baths of the mortals. It was just after noontime and all was still as I slipped between the silken sheets of cool water.

I floated a moment and then ducked under, my eyes wide open beneath the surface, and watched tiny bubbles pearl from my nostrils. I came up for air and stroked towards my favourite clump of white lilies.

How I loved to bend them forward, dip my hand into their waxy chalices and stroke the firm stamen until my fingers were coated with a powdery satin. I was exploring their slippery feel and breathing in their yeasty scent when I heard giggles.

Two servant girls from the baths on the hill were approaching my sun pool. I quickly kissed one of the lilies and dipped back into the water, my head hidden behind a curtain of willow.

'What can it mean?' one servant girl said as she sat down at the water's edge and pulled back her *chiton* to paddle her feet.

'The seed of Zeus will be born..,' said the other as she rinsed a sheer fabric.

'Of course it will,' the first said with a warm laugh.

'Don't be blasphemous,' said the other. 'It is said that his seed will spell his demise,' she added and proceeded to spread the sopping cloth in the sunshine.

'Only if it is a man,' said the other, lying back on the mossy shore. 'There was a man today ...'

'There were many,' her friend said. 'How many did you do?'

I, too, had heard the oracle, but it was a sacred thing, a matter for the gods, not for nymphs, and no matter for mortals. How could these girls speak in this way of great Zeus?

The girls' heads came together and they seemed to be whispering, their giggles pop popping gently like bubbles.

I strained to hear more, but to no avail, for to come closer would betray my presence. So I closed my eyes to imagine what they might have been saying.

I admit that mortals and their primal needs, so similar, in a way, to those of the gods, did fascinate me. The gods, too, I thought, might sometimes have wished to enjoy moments less marked by the epics, which by nature were their lot.

What could be more natural, I reasoned, than to still my curiosity by observing the mortals in a habitat close to my own? What could be more propitious than the baths on the hill? The bathhouse had often afforded me much pleasurable time as it was there that I would secretly watch the men congregate.

The women, like the two I had been watching, would serve the men as though they were gods. Young women with slender ankles like my own would undulate in sheer *chitons* by the edge of tiled pools. After bathing in the warm limpid waters, the men beckoned them. With the fleeces of young lambs, the women would dry the men's bodies and caress and massage their strong torsos until they glowed with a warm bronze patina.

Their ministrations completed, the women withdrew for a time and on returning bore platters of sweetmeats, shellfish, and olives, grapes and slices of plump pomegranates. And they would feed their masters the tasty morsels and pour them black wine, a liquid more potent than the ambrosia of the gods. Then they sang and danced seductively until the men reached for them and drew them close to partake of fervent couplings.

When I opened my eyes from this reverie the two servant girls had gone; the sheer fabric they had left behind, no doubt to finish drying in the sun.

Overcome by a new and strange need, I suddenly longed to go with them, even substitute myself for one of theirs. I had learned much from my observations, but it was not enough my curiosity told me as it now drove me forward. So I took the cloth, still damp, draped it over my breasts and knotted it in my nape.

By the time I arrived at the baths' shady portico, my covering was dry. I glanced down a moment to smooth it and saw how proudly my darkened nipples wore the attire, curious, too, in their own thrilling way.

Past the portico in a central courtyard, two men were sparring. Their bodies gleamed with sweat through caked patches of dirt and their breathing was quick. The two servant girls approached and I hid behind a sculpted pillar. With a curved metal implement they scraped the dirt-clogged oil from the men's bodies. Judging by their low moans of pleasure, the men were enjoying these attentions. Then the servants plucked fleece-like towels from a basket and led the men to the next segment of the baths. Discreetly, I followed.

Now immersed in steaming tubs, the men stretched languorously, sighed and soon closed their eyes. The warm air was drenched with the scent of olives and sweet sour excretions. So drowsy had the men now become that this must have signalled the servants to retire until further need.

Furtively, I followed the women into the next part of the baths. It was a spacious closed-in arena with an elongated pool in its centre. A man languidly parted the water as he swam. Deciding that I would be less conspicuous if I did not try to hide, I slowly skirted the walls. They were adorned with mosaics and paintings depicting the play of nymphs and satyrs. The ceiling was high and vaulted and the soft marbled hues of salmon and green recalled the subsurface life of my pool in the glade. The air was still warm, but it was imbued with a delicious new fragrance of jasmine and musk. The lap lapping of the swimmer, the intoxicating closeness of the humid air made me dizzy with a hitherto unknown form of arousal.

'You are new here,' said a man I had never before seen and grabbed at my wrist. I wriggled free, then, calming, said, yes, it was so.

'Come dry me then,' he said.

He was tall and strong, his head a mass of golden curls. His beard likewise. His lips were full and generous and his eyes were the colour of midnight.

I quivered on seeing droplets of water trickle down his firm chest past his hipbone to disappear into more golden curls of a coarser nature. A crown of fresh ivy dipped from his fingers, but I was too taken to wonder at that.

He motioned me away from the pool to a high bench of marble that gave out on a vista of olive groves. 'I am waiting,' he said as he lay down and closed his eyes.

I could but comply. So I took the fluffiest of fleeces and proceeded to blot his body…his chest, his torso and down to his thighs where an appendage I hitherto had not seen from this distance stiffened and proudly grew. I knew it to be named phallus, but the veins, barely visible, seemed to net his whole being. I drew back. The man laughed and rolled onto his stomach, exposing the tightest of buttock mounds.

'Proceed,' he said with a warm roll to his voice.

No longer having his gaze to contend with, I looked about me. Apart from one or two benches on the other side of the pool where women rhythmically attended to their masters, the baths were empty save for the lone swimmer. The only sounds were the dampened echoes of soft moans and sighs, and the fresh gentle slapping of water against the green mosaic of the pool.

Entranced, I poured virginal oil scented with olives into my palms and commenced my first massage. I drew up my robe and climbed onto the bench, my knees astride him, and let my weight guide my long strokes. His muscles relaxed under my hands. The effect seemed to please him, and this was borne out by his words, 'How good that does feel', to which I could but return my own murmur of pleasure, and proceed.

After a time, during which I addressed his back and buttocks, I alighted, came around to his head and massaged his upper back and shoulders. Perspiration trickled between my breasts, blotting the sheerness of my covering. The man's spine made me think of the central strong vein in a leaf of ivy and I could not help tracing a finger along its course.

Suddenly, through the fabric of my apparel, he lightly stroked my stomach. Thrills feathered through me. Then he reached for my buttocks and held them, not fiercely but with a firm touch. I heard the silence of strings, that silence before a tone is sounded, and pretending that I had not noticed, I proceeded to run my hands along his arms, ending with his hands and the tips of his fingers, and hoping he would not sense my own fingertips tingling.

During the course of these ministrations in which all sound dissipated I encountered the strange sensation that he was opening his mind to me, that I might even be able to enter his thoughts, perhaps read them; a prospect, which could but thrill my curiosity. The waters of my birth having taught me the need of giving myself to the flow, I applied more oil to work on his legs as I had seen the servant girls do.

I was standing at about the mid of the bench when I felt a light touching of my own legs through the folds of my covering. I felt his touch on my inner thighs. Again, his mind seemed to open and I became privy to secret thoughts of what I perceived to be a dilemma, arising perhaps from a conflict between the needs of his mind and that of his phallus, now speaking out the most primal of needs, one I, too, had to admit. Yet, he seemed governed by a singular code of civility, perhaps even good manners, since he did not demand with the force I had seen used by other men in the baths. Given his sighs and the words in his mind, this dilemma must have steered those moments of waxing and waning of the precious appendage. I concentrated on attuning my mind to his thoughts: Was she ruled by a master? Where did she live? She was new here. Not experienced. Somehow ruled by an innocent passion. Delightful.

Puzzled, yet touched by this internal conflict, I untied the knot in my nape and let my clothing slide to the floor. Then I climbed back upon the bench to attend to his legs. After some time I then turned and could not resist tantalising him by running my nipples, like fingers, up and down his back.

Eventually I climbed down and worked more on his legs. Now running my hands more lightly than before, I brought my fingers along the insides of his thighs and, making the slightest, briefest contact, ran a fingernail over the scrotum. Every fibre of his being seemed concentrated on that one area, and this slightest of attentions had a great effect, apparent from an accelerating stiffening. That stiffening now dispelled the former waxing and waning which, no doubt, had been due to the physical experience vying with a succession of random thoughts. But those thoughts had related to my own being, and I could only feel tenderness for this mortal and so, needed to speak. Yet all I could say was: 'Will you now want to turn over?' He did so, with alacrity and I knew I must change my approach.

I lightened my strokes and centred them on the tops of his thighs and lower abdomen, carefully skirting that other brain already awaiting a life of its own. My charms were now fully within reach and the man had free range of my breasts, should he so desire. And desire he did and did proceed with distinct pleasure to stroke and to tease them, to which ministrations my nipples answered with their own stiffening.

In due course my hands, fresh-slicked with oil, brushed more and more frequently, always slowly, sensuously, against scrotum and phallus which I must now call cock, so proud did it stand, enough to put any dawn rooster to shame. Thus far silence had reigned, but then he said: 'You are very, very good'. This pleased me, which he must have seen in the way I gently pursued my actions. And so his own hands now became alive, one taking increasing, almost feverish interest in my labia, gathering moisture thereupon, penetrating, exploring my clitoris (which could not help swelling), and then once again a mind intrusion: 'How often is she prone to such arousal?

What is the effect upon her? Does she even notice? Perhaps it is just how her body attends to business.

To block out his thoughts, my hands became more purposeful, still moving slowly but with deliberation. How I longed to take the luscious tip into my mouth, but I did not, as I could not dare.

Presently, his body took on a curious syncopated rhythm of its own, a kind of instinctive reflexive movement overwhelmed, one clearly destined for the procreative act. I watched enthralled as this display inexorably led to a coming of the juices of his own type of ambrosia, a coming which his mind showed me was in itself equal to that of more preferred circumstances. My pulse throbbed as my own dreams of such circumstance battled the folly of being locked in as a servant.

With a release of the hand, I slowly, gently, brought things to an end. 'I shall fetch a hot towel,' I said leaving him on his back, smiling and visibly satisfied.

My thoughts were in turmoil and in need of examination as I plucked the fabric from the marble floor, slipped it on and knotted it once more. How could I dream of more from this mortal? Would my life change back at my pool now that I knew this new hunger?

When I returned he was almost in slumber so I ministered tenderly, intending soon to depart, but knowing that I needed to leave him clean and with comfort, a comfort that I had no right to know. Then he spoke: 'Bring me food and the sweetest of wines now.'

Relieved in a way from a certain thrill, and with the feeling I might still prolong my sojourn, I left to do his bidding. I returned with a pitcher of black wine and a platter of fresh abalone, the most delicate of shellfish that like all of their kind had a hidden pearl. I also brought olives, and the shiniest reddest grapes I could find.

'Peel me one,' he said.

So I sat by his side and gingerly peeled the membrane from the plump fruit, exposing its glistening succulence.

'Feed me,' he said, and I complied. His lips closed over my fingers as he drew the naked grape into his mouth - it was almost as if to feed upon me. We continued thus until the silver platter was spent. Then he drank from the wine. When he was sated he reached for my hand. I trembled, but he insisted.

And so he led me to a canopy in a secluded corner of the baths. Parting a long curtain, he revealed a broad low couch covered in silks of the greens and the blues of my pool in the glade.

He drew me close and his fingers stroked the knot at my nape. I remained still, my heart thrilling as his hands explored the secrets of my untouched body through the folds of the fabric still covering it. He cupped my breasts, plucked at my nipples, squeezing with the gentlest of forces that transported me with shivers of delight. Although he had just eaten, his lips seemed possessed of a hunger I wished was now ready to feed upon me. His curious fingers continued their descent to find my nectar waiting to drip. He moaned in approval and I closed my eyes. And then that which was the proud cocking appendage proceeded to thrust and to pump, swallowed in full by my ravenous vulva.

As he peeled back my clothing I once again heard his mind: I saw how he felt the silk of my skin, inhaled me, visually bathed in my curves and the contrast of my pale breasts, the madder areoles. And tasting his lips, his tongue, all for me, too, became a wild dream coming true.

Enveloped by sweet sounds of a breeze swishing through willows and the lap-lapping of the nearby pool, the warm scent of sweet ginger joining musk and jasmine, I found myself totally within the moment, without past or future, my being centred in all my senses.

We trailed kisses over each other, and at last I took him into my mouth, where I held him, sucked, licked and drank him. And, like a hummingbird feasting on honeysuckle, he then dipped his tongue into me.

And so we touched and tasted our way to the moment at which I had to beg him to enter which he, wholly possessed, did, although at first with restraint. He just nudged between my labia, rubbing, tormenting me, and as I ached and urged to have him within me, he plunged deep. Then he tantalized, teased, his strokes building exquisite tension and to pre-empt surely an untimely explosion. Yet all was imbued with a charming but woeful innocence.

My fingernails scored his back, my hips thrust; I wailed and, unable to hold back any longer, his pace frenzied. I felt him swell within me, and then the hot bursts of his seed irrupted, then slowed, and he became still, still tumescent, and we both, almost still, too, panted just slightly, sweat dewing our faces, conjoining our skin as we lay together. And in that moment, as his senses retreated, faster even than his quiet dissipation, past and future suddenly blended.

'Delightful servant,' he moaned.

And I, no longer able to maintain my subterfuge, whispered: 'Dear mortal, dear mortal.'

And it was this chance remark that, as I read it, forced his vision of me, his goddess, to be in reality no such thing at all. I truly felt thus as I saw worry and fear, yes, disillusionment even, now crowding pell-mell into the mental vacuum of our spent lust. Suddenly I yearned to go back in time to the point at which he had given in to that most urgent signal of his procreative organ.

He pulled back, saying nothing, and gazed into my eyes.

Quietly, I said: 'I am, dear mortal, not the servant you think.'

Yet he did but smile and then kiss me. 'And I, dear being, am but the god Zeus.'

I pulled back.

'I also enjoy the sports of the mortals,' he said as he stroked my cheek. 'You now, dear being, you carry my seed. And that is your due, for I have opened to you the secrets of my mind.'

My senses atumble, it was then that I recognised the thrust of the oracle and how I had become its treacherous instrument.

'Dear Zeus. It must not be. Thy seed grows within me to overcome thee.'

Zeus gazed at me and with a broad palm stroked my hair. 'I am smitten by you and you have been honest with me. And yet ...' He kept stroking but I could only tremble. Then he smiled. 'I may have a solution,' he said. 'But first I must once more drink of your ambrosia.'

I did not fully understand what he meant, but when his hands resumed their gentle ministrations, when he parted my legs and nuzzled my core, his lips suckling, sucking, the delight of his tongue and his fingers probing my innermost reaches, I was once more fully transported into the flow of another life.

***

When I came to my senses, I was within him, swallowed into the belly of Zeus. No longer would I be able to delight in our couplings, but for this I had been ready to pay the price.

The oracle, I knew, could now not come true, for his seed, no longer only within me, was now within him. He would have, I foresaw, his own share of suffering.

His head, captive of the worry he tried to control, would be beset by most terrible pain. The Titan, Prometheus, would strike his cranium with one mighty blow and a goddess in the likeness of Zeus would emerge, fully clothed, clad in armour, but of a beauty quiet and firm. She would be just and she would be fair, as her father was unto me. She would be well versed in the weaving from fleeces and would prepare the most delicious of meals. All this and more would be Athena, the fruit of our coupling in the baths of the mortals.

And I, the nymph, Metis, no mortal, no goddess, would outlive Hera, the wife of his life. I would outlive all those he pursued in search of the bliss for which I was the keeper. I would remain deep within him, forever close to the heart and never far from the mind of my lover, the mighty god, Zeus.

Butter Cup

It was her friend, Elfriede, who gave her the idea. Elfriede was 79 and had just published her—some would say shocking, others erotic—autobiography, and to critical acclaim.

Martha was only 72, still attractive with her short grey hair and a figure, once sporty but now pleasantly plump. But she was not about to play an aging cougar, although Elfriede was not really a cougar, she was just a woman who hadn't been able to get to sleep. It was Elfriede's doctor who'd started it all and refused to prescribe her medication, but instead told her to get herself a man. Have sex. So Elfriede put ads in the paper and vetted her prospective lovers by phone and in interviews. She preferred them gentlemanly, fit, single and young. And she wrote about it. 'Why don't you try it,' Elfriede said as she sipped coffee in Martha's kitchen.

'I have a man,' Martha said. 'But how to get to sleep when he's snoring all night.' If I don't fall asleep before he does, Martha thought. It's a lost cause. 'There's always our goodnight kiss,' she added, but admitted to herself that over recent years it had become more of a peck.

Elfriede finished her coffee and prepared to leave. 'Have you read my book?'

'Not yet,' Martha said and leaned forward to kiss her friend goodbye. Elfriede just smiled.

Martha and Robert had been married for almost 50 years. They hadn't noticed age creeping into their joints or into his hairline, or if they had, it was laughed off until the day Martha said: 'Not as supple as I used to be.' Robert just nodded.

Sex wasn't something they did anymore, which Martha put down to their increasing plumpness rather than their age. They both had two mattresses on their beds to make things easier when they got in and out. Martha had started to cut her toenails with one foot on the toilet bowl, Robert began going to a lady down the road who would cut his.

'Pedicure,' he said.

Although Martha didn't doubt him, she did have small visits from the little green monster. And of course, that made her think of sex and Elfriede's autobiography, which she began to read.

I really don't want another man, she thought, but I could pretend. So while Robert was at his pedicure, she would play what-if? Questions danced in her mind, starring old would-be lovers and what they might be like now She would lower the curtains and lie on her bed, solving her initial lubrication difficulties with a generous dab of butter she had put into a little pot on her bedside table, just as Elfriede had advised. She would close her eyes and with one hand stroke her breasts. She would dip two fingers into the butter and then into that neglected place between her legs and gently massage the soft skin. Nerve endings responded and she would sigh. Use it or lose it, she thought. She found sex for one quite satisfying, but she wanted to share with a real live man, not any man, just Robert.

'Don't you feel like it anymore?' she asked one night as they got under their separate covers.

'Hmmm. Good night, love,' Robert said and leaned over to kiss her cheek.

'Is there something wrong with me? Am I too fat now?'

'Hmm. I'm fat, too, love. Sleep well.'

'Don't you miss it?'

'Go to sleep.'

'Robert what's wrong?'

'I can't get it up. We're too old.'

No, we're not, Martha thought. And it doesn't matter what we look like when we are … 'fucking'. There, she'd said it.

Robert was snoring.

Robert came home from his checkup with some little blue pills. 'Just samples,' he said.

Martha had perfected her sex-for-one technique, had explored her crevices with her fingers and even a hairbrush handle, but the latter felt dead. She would take a mirror and open her vulva, look inside. Like Amazon, she thought and giggled. What she enjoyed most was what her fingers did with her little pot of butter. She hid the pot behind her nighttime books-to-read pile, had it always ready to satisfy her new need. But what she wanted so dearly was to share, and she was ready. Elfriede was right. Age wasn't the problem. It was all in the mind. But Robert refused to take the little blue pills. 'Must have lost them,' he said when she asked where they were.

'You're scared.'

'Hmmm. Guess I am.'

'Can't we play?'

'Go to sleep, love.'

'I've been reading a book,' Martha said. 'A true story.'

'Hmm.'

'About a woman. She was 79 when she had sex again. We're only in our early seventies.'

'I can't, love.'

'Do you want to?'

Robert was snoring.

When Martha announced that Elfriede was coming to stay for the weekend and that she would put one of her mattresses on the guest bed, Robert just shook his head.

'I don't need two,' Martha said.

'Supple again?' he asked with a tiny smile.

'She's knocking 80,' Martha said with a straight face. Elfriede, she knew would not mind the extra height. Who knew what she might even get up to. Martha imagined Elfriede with one leg on the top mattress, her labia spread brazenly. Yes, she'd have one of those electric massage wands doing its magic over her clit, pushing inside her, vibrating, making her come. I could never do that, Martha thought, not with Robert feeling as he did, even though, as Elfriede said, these things were just toys. 'And she's written a book,' Martha added and gave Robert a wink. 'A how-to.'

Robert looked somewhat puzzled.

'I can show you some time,' Martha said, almost sulkily.

'Hmm,' Robert said. 'Can't imagine.'

When Elfriede rang to say she couldn't make it after all, that something had come up that she couldn't refuse, Martha had visions of her friend lounging in a large four poster bed, veiled only by sheer tissue and waiting, waiting, waiting for a good fuck. It was then Martha decided she herself would no longer wait. She would bathe and pamper herself, perhaps light some incense. No. Things had to be just as usual. At least, no incense. Just her butter pot. And she would pleasure herself, next to her husband just one mattress higher. She suddenly found the thought of a secret coming, right there next to him, slightly thrilling and even naughty. She might even leave just the one mattress on her bed for ever, if it felt like that. If he noticed her, why it would be a bit like a voyeur, look don't touch, his own private peep show. Martha smiled. The places you could go in your mind.

That evening while Robert was ensconced in his snoring, Martha's hand sought her own now familiar core. Spent, she turned her head towards Robert. His eyes were open. He stretched out one arm and caressed her breast. 'Go on,' he said. Martha dipped a finger into the little pot of butter on her night table beneath Elfriede's book and proceeded to pleasure herself, looking shyly at Robert, who now lay on one side. With her free hand, she lifted his duvet.

'Somebody's stirring,' she murmured. On her knees now, she took Robert's hand and guided it into her. He took up the motion, gently exploring her buttery wetness until he found, hiding, the little pearl he gladly would suckle. Sighing, Martha stroked his cock. It responded with a slight stiffening. She bent further and took it gently into her mouth, while pushing her cunt down on Robert's hand. She proceeded to lick his cock, flicking her tongue over his growing bulb, one hand fondling his balls, the other holding his cock in place. Then she sucked and sucked until her mouth was filled with a creamy sop which she slowly swallowed. It was her first time. It wasn't bad.

'Supple one, come to me,' Robert groaned.

Martha was tingling. He had come. In her mouth. She had liked it. And he wanted her. With one knee on her mattress just below his, her leg propped over his head, she straddled him, opening her vulva with one hand. Robert's tongue then explored her folds, and when he found her pearl, he suckled. Martha was wet, so wet. He gently inserted a finger and then withdrew it. 'My darling butter

141

cunt,' he whispered. Butter cup, she thought as she bent to kiss him, her buttocks raised; and as they kissed, long and languid, he stroked a finger down to her butthole, gently eased into her orifice and then withdrew. Martha was trembling. Her knees couldn't hold her anymore. She rolled from him down onto her mattress.

'Let me lie with you,' Robert said, and rolled down beside her. They lay in each other's arms, together on her mattress, and fell asleep. The only noise Martha thought she heard Robert make was a whisper of words tapering off: 'We need to get some more butter for my little butter...'

ABOUT THE AUTHOR

AstridL lives in Vienna and writes stories

http://astridL.blogspot.com